RACHEL FERGUSON

(1893–1957) was born in Hampton Wick, daughter of a Treasury official and granddaughter of Dr Robert Ferguson, physician to Queen Victoria. The household soon moved to Kensington where Rachel was educated privately, before being sent to finishing school in Italy. On her return, she flaunted her traditional upbringing to become a vigorous campaigner for women's rights and member of the WSPU. She co-founded the juvenile branch of the organisation, wrote a play for the militants and knew the important political figures of the day, including Emmeline Pankhurst, and her daughters Sylvia and Christabel.

Her interest in theatre developed, and in 1911 Rachel Ferguson became a student at the Academy of Dramatic Art. She graduated two years later and enjoyed a brief though varied career on the stage, cut short by the First World War. It was after service in the Women's Volunteer Reserve that she began writing in earnest.

Working as a journalist at the same time as writing fiction, Rachel Ferguson started out as 'Columbine', drama critic on the *Sunday Chronicle*. *False Goddesses*, her first novel, was published in 1923, and two years later she moved to *Punch*, where her 'Rachel' column became immensely popular. A second novel *The Brontës Went to Woolworths* did not appear until 1931, but its wide acclaim confirmed Rachel Ferguson's position in the public eye. Over the next two decades she wrote extensively and published nine more novels: *Popularity's Wife* (1931); *The Stag at Bay* (1932); *A Child in the Theatre* (1933); *A Footman for the Peacock* (1940); *Evenfield* (1942); *A Stroll Before Sunset* (1946) and *Sea Front* (1954). Her talent for depicting the domestic comedy of well-to-do late-Victorian families found its clearest expression in the satirical memoirs *Passionate Kensington* (1939) and *Royal Borough* (1950), both of which draw on her childhood experiences as a resident of that area. Pianist, caricaturist and lover of cats, Rachel Ferguson's later years were dominated by devotion to two causes – decayed gentlewomen and performing animals. She was for some time President of the Kensington Kitten and Neuter Cat Club. Rachel Ferguson lived in Kensington until her death in 1957.

VIRAGO
MODERN
CLASSIC

NUMBER
279

THE BRONTËS
WENT TO
WOOLWORTHS

RACHEL FERGUSON

WITH A NEW INTRODUCTION BY
A.S. BYATT

Published by VIRAGO PRESS Limited 1988
20–23 Mandela Street, Camden Town, London NW1 0HQ

Reprinted 1989

First published in Great Britain by Ernest Benn 1931
Copyright Rachel Ferguson 1931

Introduction Copyright © A.S. Byatt 1987

British Cataloguing in Publication Data

Ferguson, Rachel
The Brontës Went to Woolworths.—
(Virago modern classics).
I. Title
823′.912[F]   PR6011.E7

ISBN 0-86068-936-0

Printed in Great Britain
by Cox & Wyman Ltd.,
Reading, Berks.

TO

ROSE GERALDINE FERGUSON

AND TO OUR " HORRY "

ABOUT WHOM WE KNOW NOTHING AND

EVERYTHING

INTRODUCTION

I READ *The Brontës Went to Woolworths* when I was far too young—or just the right age, there are two ways of looking at it—and I think it isn't too much to say that it affected the whole of my writing life. I must have been about the age of Sheil in this story, a very well-read schoolgirl whose imaginary life was considerably livelier, more populated and more interesting than her real one. I was intrigued by the title, which seemed to suggest some impossible meeting of the urgent world of the romantic imagination and the everyday world of (in my case) Pontefract High Street. The book was indeed about such a meeting— and it frightened me a little, as it might not frighten an adult reader, because it seemed to loosen reality's grip on me, and my grip on reality. (I was frightened at much the same time by the childish heroine's xieties in Elizabeth Bowen's *House in Paris*, a book out the childs-eye view written wholly for adults, h I mistook for a historical romance by Marjorie wen.) When I came to reread *The Brontës Went to oolworths* to write this introduction, I was secretly afraid that it would seem merely whimsical or fey, and slightly more incoherently, that its atmosphere of danger would have gone. It does appear now to be both whimsical and fey, but that doesn't seem to matter too badly. Its atmosphere of danger has *not* gone, but there is, to a cold critical eye, an intriguing uncertainty as to how much Rachel Ferguson knew about the dangers she and her narrator-heroine were running into. Certainly *something*, she knew, but how much?

The *Brontës Went to Woolworths* is about the imagination. It is marvellously successful because it is about every kind of imagination—from mundane tabloid-journalism curiosity to Romantic art and beyond—into the edges of the uncanny and the supernatural. It is about the two habits without which no novelist can begin or continue, however much her, or his, art may vary in scope or design. It is about persistent curiosity about details of other lives and about the invention of new worlds, new patterns. The Carne family's daily life is carried on in a kind of cheerful ghostly chatter from what they once call "the creatures"—Ironface the doll, Dion Saffyn the pierrot, Lord Justice Toddington and his wife Mildr These visitors have an energy conferred by a mixtu of vulgar *schwärmerei*, journalistic fact-finding, ve fantasy, artists' inventiveness and a fatherless famii need for a male figure of authority and comfort abou the place. What intrigued me initially about them is the fact that the Saga in which they live is a *family* structure, a shared imaginative construct. (Mine were all of their essence solitary.) In this they are obviously related to the Brontës whose nursery narrative games were the imaginative centre of their lives and the source of their art. When the Saga invades reality and Toddy enters the family life the reader feels the pure pleasure one feels at the unreal happy ending of a romance—within the covers of this book, on this stage between the beginning of the ball and midnight, you may have what you desire, what you imagine will turn out to be reality, no more, no less . . .

Deirdre, the narrator, offers a whole series of definitions of the power of the imagination in the early chapters. She is aware that she is playing with dangerous shadows, though how aware is not clear— nor is it clear how far she is distanced from Rachel Ferguson who imagined her. Deirdre has rejected a proposal because she was in love with Sherlock Holmes for whose "personality and brain I had a force of feeling which, for the time, converted living men to shadows". She goes on to make the general point that perhaps most human love is in fact an act of such imagination, "the worship of an idea or an illusion. Isn't flesh and blood the least part of the business?"

She describes also—an experience I have had, and I imagine, possibly most of us have had—the sense of the imagination calling things into being—a pub she has "made up" in a novel she is writing turns out to be solidly there in the Edgware Road. This experience of the shifting, or shifty border between imagination and fact is related to something she later says to Lady Toddington about our intermittent capacity to "remember things one never saw just as it is possible to be homesick for places one's never been to". One can, she surmises, create things by brooding on them, like the pub. This speculation later runs out into the supernatural world as she remarks that theatres, music-halls, concerts

stir me to reliving the past, and I have often come home from Que n's Hall quite furious at disagreements I had ten years ago, with people with whom I am really on the best of terms.

I suppose that nothing, no emotion, no personality, ever really dies, but hangs about in the atmosphere, waiting for one to get in touch, again, through something quite spontaneous—any medium?

"Medium" here is deliberately ambivalent, suggesting both art-forms and spiritualism. Theatres and ghosts both help to construct the imaginative tissue of this novel. If Deirdre makes things up as a novelist, her sister Katrine wants to inhabit the bright world beyond the theatre lights. Deirdre considers that Drama School is making Katrine grow up in a way that threatens their common imaginative life.

My theory is that at the Dramatic School students are encouraged to make-believe all day long, and, indeed, the atmosphere there is the most unreal and artificial one I have ever breathed . . . And this has the effect of sending girls home spent with pretence and with nothing for their families but themselves to offer.

But theatres are the stuff of the Saga too, from Ironface's music-hall songs in French, to the old puppet theatre and the world of pierrots from which Dion Saffyn comes. As a girl I couldn't grasp the *glamour* of pierrots, though I noted it was there. (Lord Peter Wimsey becomes a pierrot in *Murder Must Advertise* and the elegance of the harlequinade permeates much of Marjorie Allingham's glittery, clever, warm inter-war world.) I think the television may have killed it for us—they existed, these creatures, I now imagine, in *another* light, in *another* space, across the uncrossable threshold of the footlights, unless you called them up in your own domestic surroundings and made them real . . . Freddie Pipson, the low comedian and Nature's Gentleman, who gives Katrine a job, presents a problematic aspect of the crossing of this uncrossable barrier becoming all too real, with low speech habits and unacceptable relations called Sydney who say "Haow" and "Naow" and live at Herne Hill.

It is when Katrine is leaving with Pipson and his troupe that the one-line comedian appears who keeps uttering his one line "I want to *know* when I'm dead." This joke connects the theatre subtly with the whole world of ghosts and revenants which surrounds the

worlds of the story of the novel, real and imagined.
Sheil converses (only for a sentence) with elementals
in Scotland. Father returns on All Souls Eve (why
only once? Deirdre asks, matter-of-fact masking the
plaintive, or even the need). The Brontës are aroused
by table-turning in Yorkshire and visit, with distress-
ing results, in London. Toddy opines that they envy a
family happiness they did not know. Sheil is
terrified—and here is one of the places where alarm
at the uncontrollable nature of the unreal or the
uncanny takes over from the "internal lark" of ima-
gining. It is Lady Mildred—and Woolworths—those
bastions of the everyday and the immitigably solid
who find the solution to the fear of the Brontës.

The Brontës, besides being woven into the theme
of imagined lives, also connect to the areas of
imaginative failure in this novel, which are all connected to the governesses. The Brontës, of course, as
well as being great imaginers were savagely indignant
failed governesses. Rachel Ferguson and Deirdre
know this perfectly well but it is here that the ele-
ments of moral, or emotional uncertainty that I
mentioned earlier come in. The Carnes hate having
the governesses in the house—an emotion natural
enough in anyone living in a small nuclear family who
has to make allowances for the feelings of someone
who is neither servant nor family. The Carnes are
snobs. "We are both born snobs and disbelieve in

marrying out of our class" Deirdre writes to Katrine,
à propos of Freddie Pipson, and I remember as a
child wanting desperately that true love should
triumph and Deirdre be proved wrong. I remember
too feeling a shiver of distaste for the certainty with
which the charming Deirdre dismisses Lady Toddington's coffee. "I said that I was enjoying my coffee
which was a lie. It was a good blend but servant-
made." Her attitude to the governesses is rather
similar. She despises their vocabularies and habits of
mind. They come to stand for the forces of dullness
and nullity that oppose the life of the imagination.
"Why must children have governesses? They trample,
in their business-women's shoes, upon a thousand
delicate flowers a year, and sow such boulders in
exchange."

The poor governesses, in their different ways,
excluded from the stream of invention and brilliant
chatter, pursue faintly, feel excluded, or more omin-
ously, try to join in, nearly collapsing the whole
fragile pleasure-dome. I *think* our sympathy is meant
to be with the sensitive Carnes and against the governesses, fat white women walking through fields in
gloves, to a woman. But, both as child and adult, I am
agonised by their predicament. And they do have the
sympathy of the threatening and censorious Miss
Bell.

Deirdre, criticising debutantes, "hard-eyed girls

who do all the right things and don't speak our language at all" is told by her mother "These girls have no shadows". She manages herself to reduce Miss Martin to even less than that. She considers herself to be able to imagine Miss Martin by sympathy.

The devil of it is that her home is in Cheltenham, and I once spent a day there and picked up its vibrations in no time and remember it photographically, and now the Martin has planked down her dreadful family in frames and my sympathy is going out to her quite against my will, in streamers, like seaweed. It's a horrid nuisance.

She takes up *Jane Eyre* (a warning surely?) and watches Miss Martin "in one of her quenched hats" set out with Sheil for a walk. Later, she decides in effect that Miss Martin does not exist. "I sought her company. But the creature, cornered, simply isn't there. Oh, well, I understand. Oh, how I understand!"

Does she? Poor Miss Martin is heavy-footed and heavy-handed. Her prose is dull and her aspirations—marriage with a kind-hearted curate, the holding-together of her indigent family—are made by Deirdre to seem comic or ludicrous. But she has her own sections of the narrative, free from Deirdre's voice, where she says certain things that need saying. She writes to her sister about Sheil

I shall have to be extra careful to be *commonplace* and try to bring her to see that there is plenty of mirth in *everyday* things—more than in fanciful things which never could possibly happen.

This is unintentionally humorous—poor Miss Martin could never be anything other than commonplace—but I believe it also tells a truth the story needs for balance. This truth is reinforced when for a moment we read her inner thoughts of hatred and frustration as she talks to Mrs Carne. "You are a fool and your children are liars . . . You are undermining my work and encouraging senseless delusions." Is this the sane voice of Enobarbus, cutting the flights of romantic imagination down to size? I fear it isn't. But *the Brontës* are troubled by Miss Martin's predicament as the Carnes are not. They do in a sense rescue her. What are we to make of that?

In 1967 I published a novel, *The Game*, about two sisters who were destroyed by a fantasy life which invaded or infested the real world and got out of hand. I mention that now because it is only as I write this introduction that I realise how much that novel—and much of the rest of my work—owes to the delicacy and *variety* of Rachel Ferguson's exploration of the edges of the real and the dreamed of, or the made up, or the desired. In that novel I used Dr Johnson's telling phrase about "the hunger of the imagination that preys incessantly on life". It could be argued that the Brontës were destroyed—as well as

triumphantly enlivened—by such a hunger. Muriel
Spark, on the other hand, wrote of the "transfigur-
ation of the commonplace". This is what the novel—
as opposed to the Romance—does at its best. This is
why Toddy nearly betrays himself by fantasising
about feasts of grapes from the Hampton Court vine
and red satin pyjamas with two rows of gold buttons.
What Sheil wants him to tell her is the *truth*—"some
are lavender, some are green"—"Katrine thinks they
come from Swan and Edgar"—"silk in the summer
and silk and wool in winter". These are his common-
places transfigured by her imagination, and that is
why this book manages to remain in the domain of
realistic comedy, for all its threat of whimsy at one
extreme and spiritual violence at the other. I wrote
that the good novelist needs two qualities—curiosity
about this world and the power to invent others. Miss
Martin's commonplace is not transfigured by that
curiosity which *is* a form of the imagination. The later
Miss Ainslie tries, at the other end, to diminish the
imagined world with vulgar fantasy, which is
imagination as invention, but not *alive*. Sheil tells
Toddy, during the pyjama conversation "*Our* things
aren't interesting, you know." But when the real
Toddington voluntarily involves himself in the fictive
Saga it is a true meeting of worlds—curiosity and
invention, Woolworths and the Brontës. Their things
become interesting. At the moment of that meeting

Sheil regards Deirdre with awe. "To her I knew, I had already taken on the quality of dream. I was merging into the Saga, and she, fascinated, bewildered, was watching me fade." But when Deirdre comes back from the impossible meeting, she is able to report, excited and matter of fact, the coalescence of two worlds. "Toddy," she tells them, absurdly, truthfully, splendidly "is very like himself." The pleasure of that recognition is the essential pleasure of reading novels—and part of the imagined pleasure to be got out of writing them.

A. S. Byatt, London, 1987

CHAPTER I

HOW I loathe that kind of novel which is about a lot of sisters. It is usually called *They Were Seven*, or *Three—Not Out*, and one spends one's entire time trying to sort them all, and muttering, "Was it Isobel who drank, or Gertie? And which was it who ran away with the gigolo, Amy or Pauline? And which of their separated husbands was Lionel, Isobel's or Amy's?"

Katrine and I often grin over that sort of book, and choose which sister we'd be, and Katrine always tries to bag the drink one.

A woman at one of mother's parties once said to me, "Do you like reading?" which smote us all to silence, for how could one tell her that books are like having a bath or sleeping, or eating bread—absolute necessities which one never thinks of in terms of appreciation. And we all sat waiting for her to say that she had so little time for reading, before ruling her right out for ever and ever. And then Katrine blinked at the woman and said, "Yes, a little." And had she read the latest Ruck, and wasn't it a pretty tale?

Katrine is great fun when she chooses, and gets no end of laughs out of the Dramatic School where she is studying. The course appears to consist of doughnuts and pickles and tongue in the basement, saying "Oo-er" in the Voice Production class, and floods of tears at being given the Nurse instead of Juliet at the term-end shows. Poor Katrine is absolutely sick of elocuting indecencies, and always says that when anybody gets taken pornographic in Shakespeare's plays, the part is allotted to her automatically. We hope it will break her in for the time when she plays in drawing-room comedies in the West End. Mother and I often get a rise out of her when we meet suddenly, and say:

> "Pox! how my guts do boil!"

or,

> "Now by my morning sickness! I have lost
> My virtue to this rude and rammish clown."

And once mother forgot, and when there were people to dinner called out to Katrine, "Well, my lamb, how many times did you mislay your virtue this morning?"

We often wonder what Katrine's future will be, and I suspect it will be matrimony, or tours that land up on the West Pier at Brighton.

Most of the students seem to go one way or the other.

At school, Katrine and I were much worse stage-struck than anybody. We loved certain actors and actresses so that life was a misery, and Katrine got turned right out of a history class once for kissing a post card of Ainley and murmuring, "My dear love!" And glorious was her martyrdom that night, with Henry under her pillow, if I know the business.

She certainly has enterprise, for about a year ago, when she was in the thick of a passion for an actor who lives quite near us, she went up to him in the street, beaming, and said, "Now *don't* say you've forgotten me!" And the actor peeled off his homburg and glove and cried heartily, "Well, well, well, this *is* charming." And Katrine, in great detail, reminded him of the tour of *Eastern Gods*, and (plunging) said wasn't that week at Bradford the limit? And the actor said, "A hole, dear, a hole." And they fell into a perfect orgy of shop, and when they parted, he said, "By the way, what was the name, again?" And Katrine actually told him her real name, and his face lighted and he said, "Of *course*! stupid of me. Well, bye-bye, dear. Remember me to Birdie."

Katrine could do that sort of thing, although

all three of us (for I am certain that Sheil is going that way, too) learn everything there is to learn about people we love. We get their papers, and follow their careers, and pick up gossip, and memorise anecdotes, and study paragraphs, and follow their moves about the country, and, as usually happens if you really mean business, often get into personal touch with their friends or business associates, all with some fresh item or atom of knowledge to add to the heap. Katrine had never even seen *Eastern Gods*, but she knew more about it than half the chorus, and how and where it was going.

It isn't, of course, limited to actors. It may be anybody. And while it's "on" it's no joke. I resent it awfully, sometimes. It takes it out of one so. Katrine once said to me, helplessly, "*Why has one got to do it?*"

It is even apt to ruin one's summer holidays, the going away and leaving the individual in town, or with some obsession that is probably doomed. Years ago, Katrine and I used to eye the strapped trunks, and then each other, and one of us would say, "Are we all clear?" We meant, was the holiday going to be shorn of fantastic mental disturbance, and, therefore, a normal success?

and heartening, and afterwards, we lose ourselves in fat albums and old German picture-books with coloured cuts of *Henny Penny* and the pancake, and I go home simply suffocated with the feel of bygone days. . . .

But with Sheil I am able to satisfy my craving to relive the best bits of childhood. Christmas trees and stockings (though we neither of us have ever been able to believe in Santa Claus); toyshops in country towns; the look of fruit-balls in glass bottles in village shops; the delicious smell of children's parties—tulle and gauze, warm candle grease and iced cake, and soft young hair, beautifully brushed; the bitter flavour of the gelatine on crackers; penny masks and fireworks in London side-street windows, and letting off harmless "starlights" in the school-room when the governess is out of the way.

I often wonder if I am giving Sheil a fair exchange for all these things. I think I satisfy! She absolutely sees the fun of my "doing the grown-up" at her parties, and handing her cream horns; knows that I am longing for one, too, and hoping that there may be a cracker left over for me; understands my keen disappointment when name after name is called to the tree, and the lights are blown out at last, and I had nothing. The twenties aren't supposed to

Sometimes, we found conflict awaiting us, as in the Arcaly year when we both suffered a frenzy of desire to join the resident pierrot troupe, and almost projected ourselves into it by sheer concentration. And that made the return to London all wrong. But that, at least, was shared. Also, we brought Dion Saffyn, our pierrot, home with us, and established him and his wife and two daughters in Addison Road, where many and trying were their ups and downs. For gradually it appeared that "Saffy" had married above his class—a Mary Arbuthnot, only daughter of a Somerset squire, and when they fall out, she becomes stately and "county," and generally speaking, makes Saffy feel his position.

But the girls are dears. Ennis designs for a famous French dressmaker, and Pauline is secretary in Saffy's London office, and he often rings us up when Polly is being Arbuthnot, and hurries round to us to be made a fuss of. His name is Dion Saffyn, and he has two daughters, who we often saw at Arcaly, though we never traced his wife.

I wish we knew the Saffyns.

I think Katrine is working clear of it all, but I don't believe I shall ever be free.

Three years ago I was proposed to. I

couldn't accept the man, much as I liked him, because I was in love with Sherlock Holmes. For Holmes and his personality and brain I had a force of feeling which, for the time, converted living men to shadows.

After all, isn't most love the worship of an idea or an illusion? Isn't flesh and blood the least part of the business?

I'm through with Holmes now, but I often think that he and I could have hit it off wonderfully well in Baker Street, as I am not at all demanding, and rather love old clothes and arm-chairs, and silence, and smoking, and dispassionate flights of pure reason.

It was Katrine who was upset over my refusing Stuart B. She sat on the edge of the bath while I washed out gloves in the basin, and said. "If ever I have a daughter, by God! her mind shall be a perfect blank!"

CHAPTER II

IT's lovely to have a London house schoolroom, and somebody in it of sch age. To go upstairs and find Sheil over the Wars of the Roses is like stepp a new world. It takes one's disillusio like magic, and I often long for an old well, because I adore the kind of bec room they make for themselves; it alwa of mid-Victoria and the Boer War. alive in those days, but I have a ver sense of them, and I can honestly say prefer them to our Georgian times. B know a family which has an old nurse seen the boys and girls grow up into fat mothers, and I cultivate the family be having tea with Lucy. And her walls with Militia photographs, and her work a picture of the Great Exhibition on the there is a glass ball on the mantelpiec snow man in it, and you shake it and t storm of flakes and he waves his broo we have jam sandwiches which nob ever thinks of giving one, and the tea

13

be interested in tiny spangled fans and drums full of little sweets.

I spend all the time I can in the schoolroom. I even go through the lesson-books sometimes, and am really beginning to learn something at last, though the arithmetic and grammar is eternally beyond me. How right was Humpty-Dumpty to abuse words and then pay them on Saturday night! It was a really magnificent gesture, and one which slaves to split infinitives would do well to copy.

And then I play with Sheil's theatre, when she is out on her afternoon walk. Our theatre (The Diadem) long ago scrapped the fairytale nonsense-literature which is written for puppets. *I* write our plays, and we have pantomimes with genuine illusions and ballets and properties we all make. Even Widow Twankey has her two-inch handkerchief with low-comedy fingermarks on it, in indelible ink. And we have charity *matinées*, because they sound so sonorous. Sometimes we invent the charities, too, and whenever I have finished a new play some benevolence springs into being. The Tabbies Protection Union has offices in Great Cream Street, and The Insolent Widows Aid (Sheil's contribution) has premises in Crape Yard, E.C. Others include The Depressed Char-

women Society and The Nautical Sailors'
Rest. As a result of a *matinée* for the latter, we
were happy to be able to announce that our
new wing of dormitories in Chatham was now
completed, "and," chimed in Sheil, "the dear
lads can now sleep in contagious rows, freed
from the sadness of the sinful gutter." And we
have a resident ballet troupe, called "The
Kensington Palace Girls."

I often rootle in the toy-box. Mixed with
Sheil's toys are Katrine's and my own. As a
family, we have never liked dolls, never believed
in fairies and all rather hated Peter Pan. Poor
Sheil, the latest victim of the whimsical, could
make neither head nor tail of it, and the only
doll we ever unitedly esteemed was the plainest
one of the collection. Ironface. She was given
to me when I was seven. Her face and forearms
were of painted tin and she had a well-made
kid body. Ironface, unfortunately, outgrew us.
She developed an intolerably overbearing manner, married a French Count called Isidore
(de la So-and-so, de la Something Else), and
now lives in feudal state in France, whence,
even to this day, she makes occasional descents
upon us by private aeroplane-de-luxe, patron-
ising us in an accent enragingly perfect and bear-
ing extravagant gifts which we have to accept.

Me she addresses as "Ah, Trotty! *Ça marche, hein?*" She has composed two songs, both in praise of herself. The first, picturing the delight of heaven at the event of her death, began:

> The angel at the Golden Gate
> Says, "The Countess tarries late,
> *We want her hither*."

The second (immensely popular, thanks to Ironface, in the Parisian music-halls of the early nineteen-hundreds) ran:

(*Allegro vivace*)	Je connais une belle mondaine
	(Ah! comme elle est chic!)
	De costumes elle a une trentaine
	(Ah! comme elle est chic!)
(*Hold back the time*)	Quand elle se promène dans les Bois
	Ce n'est qu'un cri, "Parbleu! Ma foi!
	Regardez-moi donc cette femme-là."
(*Prestissimo con brio*)	AH! COMME ELLE EST CHIC!

This was one of my good-night songs, with mother tossing it off in the vaudeville manner at the foot of my bed; hands on hips, a rakish, challenging leer for the conductor. We sing it to Sheil, still. Ironface was lost, or given away, quite thirteen years ago, but it's no good. Like the poor, she is ever with us. We've tried, half-heartedly, to humanise the other dolls, but their characters won't emerge. They are

rather like the servants and governesses who
come and go; they won't immortalise. But
occasionally they get their own back on me.
Miss Martin has only been with us about a
month, but I rather think she is going to take
toll of me. The devil of it is that her home is in
Cheltenham, and I once spent a day there, and
picked up its vibrations in no time and remember it photographically, and now the Martin
has planked down her dreadful family in frames
and my sympathy is going out to her quite
against my will, in streamers, like seaweed.
It's a horrid nuisance. And, though we seldom
talk for long together, I already know the feel of
Cheltenham's main avenue in July, and the
way the light struck the tea-pot when, at
breakfast, Captain Martin broke it to his
daughters that they must clear out and earn
. . . and I rather think the girls dispersed about
the house and avoided talking much, that day.
But they probably met in the town. One is
always liable to run against people in stewpan
sort of places like Cheltenham. It's part of the
damnableness of it—and the fascination. Im-
provident, pathetic, reprehensible and blasted
Captain Martin! How my heart aches for him
and his heavy-faced brood. Will one never be
allowed to possess oneself in peace?

CHAPTER III

LAST summer we all went to Skye, where father was born, and I caught Katrine's eye in our hall and muttered the "all clear?" and she nodded.

The holiday was a success. The place got at me a bit, of course, but that wasn't a tribute to its quality of eerieness, for a garden suburb can do the same thing, but, that year, I had a guard, a buffer.

I've always envied those people who own a place the moment they arrive. In my own experience, new places invariably own me, until I have fought them down. I remember one summer in a furtive Gloucestershire village and how it fairly pulled me out of the train before I set foot on the platform. And it wasn't a pull of welcome.

Skye was a success for Katrine because she had just ended a term at the Dramatic School and was looking forward to the next, and for me because I was writing my first novel, so nothing could touch me very badly. Meanwhile, I was finding out that writing a book makes one singularly absent-minded, and one's

conversation boring and laboured. It's hard on
the family, I suppose, but oh! what an internal
lark! And what an escape from journalism. I
shall loathe the word "nowadays" and the
phrase "modern girl" till I am dead, and even
then my heart will hear it and beat when I'm
earth in an earthy bed. What I can never get
my editors to realise is that every soul who is
alive is "modern," and that when they use the
word they privily mean depraved or racketty.

I never knew what an extraordinary thing it
could be to write a book. In the first place, the
characters take the bit between their jaws and
canter off with you into places you don't want
and never catered for. I had smugly intended
my book to be about a family rather like ours,
but, lud love you! it's already turned into an
account of a barmaid's career in an Edgware
Road pub, and I can't squeeze us in *anywhere*!

Odd things happen, too. I had called my
pub, "The Three Feathers," and counted on
there being heaps of pubs in Edgware Road, not
called that, but looking a bit like my description.
Before we left home, I went down Edgware
Road to investigate, and found my pub, even
down to the old-fashioned phonograph on the
table in the upstairs sitting-room. And I
thought, "*I* built that place."

I wonder how much one does create by brooding over it? The family is always asking me to read them "bits," and I always refuse. The general public (if I ever have one) I don't mind a bit, but reading what one has written is like kissing a lover in a tram. Katrine agrees with me. That's why the Dramatic School is probably going to be so good for her; you have to strip yourself morally naked there.

The evenings in Skye are rather wonderful. They seem to endure for ever, like the goodness of the Lord, and when the moon is high, one can read quite clearly at midnight. But the boating round Dunvegan is tricky for the amateur because of the narrow natural arches and the submerged rocks.

I came out one night to call in Sheil, for it was long past her time for bed, but didn't appear to be, thanks to the leisured sunset, and saw her in the distance, sitting on the turf with a man, and my heart turned over. She is very pretty, and—anyway, I ran. She seemed to be enjoying herself, and she had a paper bag in her hand, the contents of which they were sharing, their heads on a level. When I reached her she was alone. And then I knew that the creature was one of those nature spirits with which Skye is teeming, and England, too,

wherever there are downs or wide quiet spaces.
Father once wrote a book about them. He once
got lost in Wales, on Cader Idris, and saw one
of the members of the little subterranean race
whose tappings have been heard by dozens of
tourists. I asked him if he was frightened, and
he said, "Oh no. I just said 'hullo,' and the
little man bowed and vanished."

But Sheil?

I lit a cigarette and said, "Saffy thinks it's
time you came in, and Polly is in one of her
Arbuthnot moods this evening."

"Oh, *why* ?"

"Because the shooting in Scotland has fallen
through, and she is loathing having to go back
to Addison Road."

"Oh, *poor* old Polly!"

"Yes. A bit thick. But if she *will* marry a
pierrot——"

"But—the Macalistairs are *fond* of Polly and
the squire! They wouldn't put her off because
of Saffy? She was to have gone on from here.
By the eleven-fifteen." Sheil's voice was almost
a wail.

"Well . . . it may be only a hitch," I con-
ceded.

"And is Toddy going to come in after his
hotel dinner?"

"Oh, yes. He met Saffy leaving our digs, and there was the usual snorting match."

Sheil's shrill giggle startled a curlew. Then Crellie bounded up to her and her attention was instantly diverted to the dog. His muzzle was slightly gory, so we knew he had been doing something forbidden in the sheep or rabbit line, and that meant his confessional vespers hymn. We chanted:

> "Four prickles to me toe,
>   Murdered innocents rahnd me go!
>   Two sheep, one duck,
>   Three cats an' a cluck-cluck."

Crellie drooped mechanically, and looked sly. He is really rather awful at times, and loves rubbing his bosom in frightful smells and then sitting in the middle of them with his head bowed, looking sacred. He is a mass of good-nature, however, and, unlike Ironface, no snob, but only rather a liar. His tiger story is of how he assisted Lord Roberts to relieve Mafeking. ("Bobs," I sez, "we've done it between us." "Colonel Crellie," 'e says, "you're a 'ero."). But we smacked him, for luck, Mafeking or no.

CHAPTER IV

I FIRST saw and spoke to Lady Toddington two years ago, though I had known her intimately for nearly three years.

A jury summons had commanded mother (on a buff slip, ending "hereof fail not," for which I forgave it everything), and I had faithfully turned out in attendance, armed with smelling-salts and meat lozenges, at nine o'clock of a misty morning. As a family we all had a horror of "the Law" comparable only to the fighting fear of "the House" that is the universal badge of every broken tramp. The Court happened to be Toddington's. My jibbing companion was not called, after all, but in spite of that she was compelled to attend as reserve for the remainder of the week. The Law can be extraordinarily insolent and ungrateful. I wouldn't treat a dog as it treats jury members it can't use up. But, meanwhile, and even as mother trembled and looked guilty and I drank in the scene, an usher was holding the curtain which was distinctly due at the cleaners' and Toddington swept in and occupied the Bench.

From that moment, I think, he owned, occupied and paid taxes on our imagination.

The obvious first move was *Who's Who*, and here I came in useful, for I filched a copy from one of my newspaper offices.

Born 1858. (*A blow, because it gave him less time to go on living.*)

Clubs: The Athenæum and the Garrick. (*Why the Garrick? It's full of actors.*)

Married (*aha!*) in 1884.

Her name was Mildred Ethelreda Brockley. (*Lor!*)

Two addresses. A riverside and town one. (*What sends him to the river?*)

A list of costly and conventional hobbies. Golf. (*The lamb! What a pet he must look in plus-fours!*)

A digest of a typical, suitable and expensive education. Two inches of spectacular legal achievement. (*Clever* boy!)

Since then, we must have walked past his house a dozen times. It didn't tell one much. I kept tally of when his window-boxes were renewed, and wished that he (or Mildred) hadn't such a passion for privet and calceolarias, but through the dining-room window I could see a very decent oak dresser, and the warming-pan on the wall looked well polished.

Photographs of him were, of course, easy to come by (two of my editors gave me three), and the family generally assumes another print on the way whenever the postman scrabbles and ends by having to ring the bell and knock twice.

The next hunt was for somebody who knew Toddington. One of my friends has a husband who "used to see a lot of him"; the husband (need I say it?) was entrenched in Kenya, growing coffee, and several other times I came similarly near the verge. My professional work I knew couldn't help. I am not a reporter. I am that rather unclassifiable creature which Fleet Street sometimes chooses to write descriptive signed articles on people and "movements." Thus I have sat for a whole afternoon upon the bed of a notorious Mormon bishop, in Tottenham, and in the Abbey on Princess Mary's wedding day. But for all that, when next in the office I suggested to my editor that something might be done.

"But why, why?" he fretted, "you can't report the cases—Henderson and Cato do those, and R. E. Corder of the *Mail* has covered all the personal stuff about the judges."

"Well, I *want* to meet Toddington," I said. "D'you *like* him?"

"I adore him," I shouted. For I discovered years ago that the best way to put people right off the scent is to tell the truth and nothing but the truth. It acts like a charm.

My editor grinned, and ran his hand through his hair.

"Well, I'm awfully sorry, but I don't see what we can do."

"Beast! Pig!" I answered (for I am sincerely fond of him).

"By the way, I'd like you to do us something bright on, 'Is the Bank Holiday Girl Naughty?' About a thousand."

"All right. I'll go in next door and write it now, if you'll lend me a pencil, paper, and a rather large basin," I agreed.

"—and don't come down too hard on Brighton. The guvnor's going there in August."

It was close on one o'clock before I had written my copy. Binton called me in, pointed to his desk. "There. You can have that. I'll get another print done for the library." He bent over the photograph of Toddington. "Ugly little beggar he is."

"Very plain," I agreed placidly, "and thank you awfully." I have discovered that it is hopeless to praise one man to another; they are up in arms in a minute, and as jealous and watch-

ful as a crowd of catty débutantes. Binton is
supposed to be very good-looking, his typist
tells me, and I've often caught sight of him
arranging his profile at the society women who
come in hoping for free publicity, but his looks
don't amuse me a bit, and never will. As far
as looks go, I honestly prefer Jelks, his sub, who
is definitely plain, and scatters his h's thick as
leaves in Vallombrosa, and says "arver" when
he means "however," and calls *Who's Who*
"Oozoo," as though it were some kind of witch-
doctor or black magic rite in Central Africa.
But they are both great dears.

When I got home the gong had just sounded
for lunch. Meals, in our family, are usually
eaten amid a cloud of witnesses, unless there are
visitors. Dion Saffyn cannot, of course, often
get away from his office, but he talks to us down
the telephone while we eat, and so does Pauline.
Infinitely more rare intrusions come from
Ironface, who has, by now, more or less
dwindled to a faint and mannered "*Tra la!
mes enfants!*" in the ether. We sometimes admit
quite openly that she is a bore. Katrine's advent
at the Dramatic School has brought her actor
friend about us, rather, and we all hope he
won't begin to try and borrow money from us.
Mother once reduced him to reciting *To Be*

Or Not To Be to the queue outside the Gaiety, but we soon rescued him from that predicament, and in his gratitude, he took to flirting with us all for a bit, turn and turn about, and calling mother, "Arrrr, dearrrr lady!" and greeting poor Sheil as "Sweet chiiiild, and how is my little maid?" with a vibrato in his voice studiously copied from the throat effects of George Alexander. But we don't make a whole lot of use of him, and Katrine, to whom he belongs if he belongs to anybody, is becoming definitely aloof. I am going to miss her horribly, but I suppose I know the reason. My theory is that at the Dramatic School students are encouraged to make-believe all day long, and, indeed, the atmosphere there is the most unreal and artificial one I have ever breathed, even when classes aren't in progress. And this has the effect of sending the girls home spent with pretence, and with nothing for their families but themselves to offer.

This morning, I took my place at table in the middle of an argument between Toddy and Henry Nicholls, his associate, as to what he should have sent in from Simpsons' for his lunch. Toddy is terribly particular about his food, and always wants a double portion of oysters in his steak pudding when he goes to

the Cheshire Cheese, and Sheil says that "he
weaves in his pudding with his little hands to
pick the oysters out first." Nicholls is devoted
to him, and they have, lately, taken to having
rounds of golf together on Saturdays, unless
Toddy is down to be Chambers Judge in the
morning. Whenever I spend a spare afternoon
in Toddy's Court and see the associate sitting
beneath him, and swearing witnesses or mount-
ing to confer with Toddy (who pretends hardly
to know him on these occasions), I smother a
grin to think of what happened say, a fortnight
ago, or yesterday. And when the court rises,
it is really dreadful to have to turn out with the
rest of the casuals into the Strand, and not to
run up (as we had arranged) to see Toddy in
his private room.

His outfit keeps us in perennial suspense.
Judges have the most amazing trousseau.
Whenever I think I have got to the bottom of
Toddy's trunk, he whips out something else and
puts it on.

Sometimes he wears black, with a red band,
or red with a black one; on other occasions he
appears in black with an ermine tippet and
cuffs, and looks like Lewis Sydney in the Follies,
and I have caught him in black tastefully lined
and relieved with beige silk and a hood tied up

with bows, and when I'd recovered from that, he toddled in next time in a very *chic* effect in pink shot silk. But I admit that his cuff-links are always the same—plain, oval, and gold. Mother says she is only waiting for him to bound in in a ballet skirt and rosebuds, and then perhaps we shall work round again to the black-and-red gown. And after that, we went upstairs and had a charity *matinée* (for the Browbeaten Barristers Benevolent Fund) in which our star doll played in a drama called *Perjured Oaths.*

Being Saturday, Katrine was at lunch too, and, suddenly, as I began to eat, deadly depression engulfed me. It sometimes does, and often quite irrationally, and one drifts with it, because fighting it is no good. Father used to be the same, and would often say how he started a day meaning to love every minute of it, but in a moment "along comes me this cursèd black pudding out of the blue, and destroys me root and branch."

I looked round the table, at Katrine, at my mother and my Sheil, at poor Miss Martin, and I thought, what the deuce are we all here for? Is mother satisfied? Am I worth tuppence? Will Sheil grow away from me and marry some cast-iron dolt? Is it conceivable that Katrine

will ever get three lines to speak on the stage?
And why must we have the Martin with us, the
tragic, blasted wretch? And why isn't Toddington here? Katrine, too, seemed rather less than
usual.

"Toddy is coming to dinner to-night,"
piped Sheil, "and we've got him lamb cutlets,
which he wholly adores. And isn't it about
time that we had Mildred too, mother?"

Miss Martin looked bright. It is the last shot
in her locker. "And who, may one ask, is
'Toddy'?" she enquired.

"Toddington," answered Sheil crisply.

Mother looked self-conscious, and I began to
think in the Shakespearean manner. It is
always soothing.

> "Out, damnèd she,
>   And from this riven house
>   Get wholly hence."

What a foul place the world was when one
stripped it bare. How remorseless and stingy,
how essentially tooth-for-a-toothish.

After lunch I inveigled Katrine into the
Middle Temple, for I thought I might as well
profit by her mood, and she was so depressed
that she strode like Mrs. Crummles, and I was
so rasped with life that I hit Goldsmith's tomb

with my umbrella. I said, "I'd give five pounds if somebody'd come along and tell us both how clever we are."

"I'd give the dustman half a crown if he'd take me away with the rest of the filth."

"I bet he wouldn't do it under three bob," I sympathised.

Then by way of cheering me up she snarled, "And we're going to Yorkshire, this summer," and we groped into a cinema because they are the most depressing places in the world, and we both believe in the principle of homœopathy.

That night I sat up late, reading. I have never met a more sympathetic library than that which father assembled. Thanks to him I discovered *The Martian* and *Peter Ibbetson*, *Wuthering Heights*, and *My Two Kings*, by Mrs. Evan Nepean, who, when she went to the National Portrait Gallery and saw Kneller's portrait of dead Monmouth, suddenly remembered that it had once belonged to her; suddenly knew her former life at the court of Charles the Second, and wrote it, in the War, and so inflamed me that I, too, have stood before the lovely, worthless James Scott, and found it one of the beautiful pictures of the world—and could remember nothing!

These faces! How they fasten on one! I

was safe, for some reason, from the fated fribble, but there are others . . . all pressing their past, their claims, all reaching out, very, very quietly, to draw one in . . . they cease to be flat surfaces and become little stages on to which one could squeeze oneself. . . .

And that scarred canvas, dismissed as "a dreadful daub" by the biographers: Emily Brontë, in stormy profile. I am no art critic, I only value in pictures that which lies beyond them. Emily managed to hurt me. She is, I am certain, harassed at her place in Trafalgar Square. When first I saw her I said, "My dear, I can't do anything about it."

I discovered Rabelais, and thought him an obscure and limited bore. I'm quite certain that if I wanted to be indecent I could be more original than that, and mother and Katrine say they could, too. And, just as I was skimming *The Wind in the Willows*, and had got to "*Handsome* Mr. Toad!" (who really has much in common with Ironface, and even with Crellie in his Mafeking moments), I got a twinge, and began to be quite certain that Miss Martin wasn't being happy. I tried to exorcise her with James's *A Warning to the Curious*, but it wasn't any real good, and I cursed, and turned out the lights, and went upstairs. And I stood outside

her door and listened. She would be crying for
Cheltenham and the Captain. There is, possibly, a desk special to her use, and a bedroom
whose every creak she knows. . . . I stood outside her door and listened: surprised at myself,
I knocked. And again.

"I—thought I heard you moving about," I
faltered, to the unalluring figure in its seemly
bedgown. And I was right. Her eyes were
pink.

"Oh . . . no. How kind of you . . . no."

Oh well . . . heaven knows I didn't want a
set piece with her on the landing.

CHAPTER V

IN the morning I woke determined to be as miserable as I was the day before, and so work through it that way, and get it all cleared up, but I found myself perfectly cheerful. I began to try and account for it, and came to the conclusion that it was because it was mother's birthday to-morrow, and Katrine's term-end show in a fortnight.

Perhaps it is because we get so few outside presents that we make such an occasion of our own. We used to get far more when father was alive, possibly because we were much younger, probably because men do bring people about the house, just as a tom cat will always attract others. Mother won't entertain alone, although she bears very nobly with what she calls "the drunks" that Katrine and I bring in, meaning young writers and students of both sexes. At Christmas and on birthdays we fairly shower presents on each other, and that, again, is another reason against having guests, because an alien shower would come too expensive. And, thinking of mother's birthday, I thumped on the wall and Katrine came in half dressed.

"Look here, old chap," I said, "about mother's birthday."

"The Martin?" guessed Katrine.

"Good woman! Katrine, I can't and won't have the things by mother's place at breakfast. D'you get me?"

"I get you. But—does Martin know it's mother's birthday? Because, if she does . . . and Sheil will be sure to have told her . . . and we can't tell Sheil *why* we don't want the things put by her place. Poor Martin hasn't many legs to stand on with the kid——"

"—one ought to leave her one. I see. Look here. *I* know. We'll all give mother *one* of our things at table—the most fetid of the lot——"

"What ho!" appreciated Katrine.

"And K., how are you off for dibs?"

"Thrift, thrift, Horatio. It'll be another month before I get m' hands on any twinkling, chinking dem'd mint sauce."

I gave Katrine two pounds because I am the man of the family now, and I sometimes feel as though she and Sheil were my daughters. At mother's place there were three small parcels, and we were so decorous at breakfast that we nearly burst, and spent the time trying not to catch each other's eye, while mother thanked us and Miss Martin looked on, poor catfish!

(She hurried out later on and bought mother a bunch of roses, and I wondered what Martin birthday mornings were like.) But we rushed mother into the drawing-room and were able to be ourselves for quite twenty minutes.

There were eleven parcels, all told. Ironface had sent a big box of Fullers' chocolates, and Crellie a glass powder-bowl with his card inside (Colonel Crellie: United Services Club). He had bought the present with his ear-money, for we think he must keep it there, as he has no pockets. Dion Saffyn had sent a stall for a play we knew mother wanted to see ("with fond love from Saffy"), and Polly a big bunch of lilies of the valley ("From my father's garden, with kindest thoughts from Mary Arbuthnot Saffyn"), so then mother guessed that Polly was in one of her County moods, and probably being a little jealous of our intimacy with her husband. Pauline and Ennis only sent cards, because it was felt that they couldn't afford presents except at Christmas, on their salaries.

But the best thing came from Toddington. Three lovely pairs of silk stockings and his card ("With very many happy returns to my dear Mrs. Carne from her old friend Toddy." Garrick Club. Athenæum), and mother hugged us all and said, "Oh *thank* you, Toddy, the old dear!"

And then she began to open our presents.

The end-of-term shows at the Dramatic School were so funny that my nose began to bleed, and I had to grope my way out and yell it off in the cloak-rooms. But mother, shuddering with giggles, sat it all out so as to be able to say what there was to say to Katrine. Her *rôles* included Polonius, and she'd just got to "costly thy habit" when her beard came half off and swung like a pendulum for the rest of the scene, and in *The Professor's Love Story* (Oh! what a bad play!) the gate stuck, and pinned that whimsical recluse to his own fence. And later on, mother told me, one of the girls (as a farmer) had to fill a pipe and smoke it, and she stuffed the bowl so full that a man in the audience said "Christ" out loud, and of course it wouldn't draw, and the girl pulled nearly all of it out again, and mother said, "The stage was knee-deep in shag. That girl ought to get on." And Toddington, sitting by mother, looked austere and tolerant, and said that these mishaps must be very trying, where all were working so hard. And afterwards, he drove us home in his car. Mitchell, his chauffeur, is beginning to know our address so well, now, that we have often noticed a slight tendency on his part to cough like a stage butler whenever it is mentioned, and once I told it as a joke to Toddy, and he was down on Mitchell like a ton of bricks. Toddy has a tongue like a whip-lash. It is only to be expected.

My novel went off to a publisher a fortnight ago, and I am cold with excitement. Toddy thinks it "exceedingly good," and said I was a clever child, and took me to the Ritz to celebrate, and made rather a stir as so many people recognised him. Mildred wasn't there. She is altogether a little unapproachable, and although she has "called," we all felt it was more or less to countenance her husband's friends.

But as time goes on—it is nearly a year, now, since the jury summons—she is gradually beginning to show us another side of herself. She drove me back, for instance, a week ago, to her house, and gave me a cherry brandy and had one herself, and suddenly kicked off her shoes and said she was sick of her life and whatever was the use of tiring oneself out in the season for a pack of people who didn't care a dump for her? And mother said, "How Toddy would loathe her saying 'whatever!' But I always told you Mildred wasn't as top-

shelfish as you think she is. After all . . .
Brockley is anybody's name."

Mother is so sane; she can always be trusted
to come out with something reassuring. Bogeys
hate her.

I said, "Then *why* did Toddy marry her?"

"Oh well, you know how it is. And he was
only in his twenties. And I expect she was
pretty."

And then I said, "*Isn't* it rum to think that
Toddy eats, and shaves and has tiny little liver
attacks?"

"But of course he does! I expect he takes pills
by the spoonful! He looks what Mildred would
call 'bileyfied.'"

"Oh, he *doesn't*!"

Mother pulled my chin. "I believe you think
he goes about on a gilded elephant."

"Well," I countered, "can you *see* him in a
train, or a bus?"

"But of *course* I can! I bet he takes buses
every day of his life."

"Well, I can't see him doing it," I answered
truthfully. And then I went into the library and
had an inferiority complex. The season was
still on, and cars were rolling by full of expensive
people who were in demand; hard-eyed girls
who do all the right things and don't speak our

language at all; who are so jolly sure of themselves, so positive about life, and whose highest tribute to joy is a drawled "Mahvellous!"

I tried to explain it all to mother, once, and she said, "These girls have no shadows."

One doesn't envy them, but one is alarmed by them, stupidity and all, and intimidated and impressed. And by they all went, doing Mildred Toddington sort of things at times dedicated by everybody else to work. But, at the same time, from about this period I date the change in Mildred. She became more human, even less bred.

And I began to read books about people whose spirits were even "lower" than mine, for that is the only possible book for these occasions, and I took down *Jane Eyre*, and watched Miss Martin, in one of her quenched hats, taking Sheil out for a walk.

But I couldn't settle to anything, and I planned to take Katrine to a music-hall in the evening. We would go to an outlying hall because the turns are always better and more virile in those places, and we both love the twice-a-night atmosphere, and the sequins that are missing from the tabs, and the hurried overture with the band wiping the beer from its lips, and the advertisements of the local

shops that the lantern in the family circle
throws on to the screen . . . ready-to-wear
trousers like drain pipes, and hats in which one
wouldn't be seen dying. And at one of the
Empires there is a grocer called Soper, who
always advertises, and when his slide comes we
always applaud, because he is probably rather
bald, and feeling his age, and bewildered by
the competition of the chain stores, and because
it is so terrible to have a surname like his.

And sometimes we go behind and talk to
anybody I know that may be on the bill. And
Katrine is all agog, and impressed with me, and
I pretend I'm not a bit, though the sight of a
dress-basket and the smell of the stone passages
always goes to my head. Katrine will grow
out of her feeling because she is only stage-
struck and inexperienced, and three weeks in
the provinces will settle her illusions for ever,
whereas I am not a bit stage-struck any more,
but the trappings will impose themselves on
me for ever, though I know them for what they
are.

We adore what we call "Hai—hup!" turns;
they are always active and all over spangles, and
one gets plenty of them in the suburbs. Katrine
is always sorry for the girl who only stands at
the back of the set in tights and looks bright and

interested, and catches things, and always
wonders what her home looks like, and what
she reads and really thinks about things. I
don't have to bother, because I've met her, and
I know she thinks of nothing but the show, and
clothes, and lucky charms and men, and that
her home is a combined room in Kennington
Road or Highbury New Park, with a cruet on
the chiffonier. Comedians are far more elastic
in their higher reaches, and think of plenty of
things, and are apt to collect artistic objects far
above their station, and are usually thoroughly
good sorts and not a bit the "laddie" type. And
this week, Freddie Pipson was topping the bill,
and I said to Katrine, "We'll go and see him
afterwards."

Pipson is a wonder. He is the only justifica-
tion I know for that dreadful phrase, "One of
Nature's gentlemen." He has everything except
birth, and if he ever marries, his wife will be a
lucky and blessèd woman. He is earning two
hundred a week and was born in the slums; his
handwriting is awful and his relatives un-
presentable, but I would trust my life, money,
and daughter to him without thinking twice.
And I thought of all that while the band blared,
and Pipson marched in in a comedy uniform,
sword and scratch wig, and sang his famous

"I'm the Captain of the Loyal Kitchen Rangers," while the house roared. He told me once that it was his landlady that gave him the idea, years ago, when he was an obscure first turn, and he wrote the chorus on an old envelope and got a try-out at Islington, "And it went so big, Miss Carne, I never looked back, and I've been singing it, off and on, ever since."

We joined in the chorus with everybody, and Pipson suddenly saw me, and saluted, and gave that imperceptible sideways nod of the head that meant we were to come round after the show.

> "I'm the Captain of the Loyal Kitchen Rangers!
> I lead the men to battle, in the rear,
> With dispatches on my cuff,
> By Jingo, I'm the stuff!
> And the foe for mercy shout
> When I pull my dampers out.
> People say, 'Who is that handsome man
> Who's standing by the butts?'
> And the privates always point me out to strangers.
> I'm the idol of the reg'ment, and I'm one of Derby's
>   nuts,
> I'm the Captain of the Loyal Kitchen Rangers!"

Pipson wrote it early in the War, when he had been rejected by three recruiting offices. He said to me that he had never been through such humiliation, and so he came home to find salvation on the back of an envelope. But the night he sang it to "real soldiers" he nearly broke down. He gave half his salary to War charities, and gave up smoking altogether, and even now only has one drink after his work is over, though his dressing-room is like a bar, for visitors. So I nodded "yes" to him. I met him first a few months ago when I was doing a series of music-hall impressions for Binton, and I couldn't get him to talk about himself because he would talk about me. Katrine whispered ecstatically, "Oh, *will* somebody say 'Pleased to meet you' to us?" "All of them," I replied, "and what the answer is, I haven't the faintest idea. It's like when people say 'God bless you'; one doesn't know whether to say 'Don't mention it,' 'Not at all,' or 'The same to you.'"

And then, while Pipson hurried off to change for his next number, while the band played the chorus of the Rangers and then broke into the chorus of the number to follow, I fell into one of those mental maunders that noise always induces, and wondered why one mustn't say "Pleased to meet you" when it expresses exactly what one wants to convey, and then the back of the conductor's head gave me the idea for a music-hall sketch, and the tune gave me the outline for a ballet synopsis—why, I can't imagine, as the music was completely unsuitable for dancers, but lights and noise are like flame to gunpowder with me, and I once planned a problem - play through watching a turn rattle out *William Tell* on the xylophone. Theatres, halls and concerts have another effect, too; they stir me to re-living the past, and I have often come home from Queen's Hall quite furious at disagreements I had with people, ten years ago, with whom I am really on the best of terms.

I suppose that nothing, no emotion, no personality, ever really dies, but hangs about in the atmosphere, waiting for one to get into touch, again, through something quite extraneous—any medium? . . .

When we had got past the Sergeant, Pipson was waiting for us outside his dressing-room in a vest, a clanless kilt and a flannel dressing-gown. He had removed his wig of Caledonian carrot and his hair was brushed and sleek. He wrung my hands and said, "This is so kind of you." And I said, "I've brought my sister."

"I'm very glad indeed. Might I ask you both to come in? Mr. Bagley, my seckertry."

"Pleased to meet you," answered Katrine, and Bagley edged out while Pipson brought us cushions and footstools, and offered us whisky, brandy, port, gin and angostura and cigarettes, while his two dressers tried to take his spats off.

"Now, never mind about the time, I'll drive you home. Well now, how's the work? I read your article on this Bastardy Bill with very great interest, and I'm with you, in the main, about everything you say. This class of kiddy . . ."

Ten minutes later he flung a greasepaint-smeared towel aside and said, "I wish you'd write me a new number, Miss Carne. I'm not getting this Scotch one over."

"No. I noticed that."

"You did?" He turned to Katrine. "I'm always grateful to people like your sister who'll tell one the truth, Miss Carne. I went rotten to-night, and I know it." And to me, "Well, what about it?"

I shook my head. "I haven't the touch. I should be either much too refeened or so low you couldn't sing it."

"What a joke, eh?" He looked at Katrine with his sad, monkey eyes. "It may seem odd to you, Miss Carne, but I never sing or say a line I wouldn't sing or say before you." And to me, "Well, dear, do think it over."

"Let's write it now!" said Katrine. Half a small glass of port and the proximity of Pipson

were too much for her. "We'll take a line
each."

"I am going to ask you to forgive me while
I change," and Pipson went into his inner
room.

"All right."

"You begin, dear."

"Play fair," I objected, "You'll have to do
your bit, change or no."

I considered the rows of greasepaints on his
dressing-table.

"*I'm engaged in shaving scooters for the pips they
put in jam*," I sang.

"That's torn it!" called out Pipson, throwing his kilt through the door, and added, in his
tenor,

"*And I chip the ice from mutton that I sell as
English lamb.*"

"*I'm a pillar of the chapel ev'ry Sunday, yes
I am!*"

"*And whatever should I do without me con-
science?*" chirped up Katrine.

Pipson put his head through the door, serious
at once. "That's a little controversial, Miss
Carne, if you know what I mean. I'm Church
of England, myself, but we've got to respect
what other people believe in. So many people
in my audience are Chapel, you'd be surprised."

I saw that in another second Katrine would explode, but luckily Pipson's chauffeur looked in and intimated that he was due at the Shepherd's Bush Empire in half an hour, and Pipson crated us in his enormous Daimler as though we were glass, or a loan collection of Flemish pictures, and said, "Night, Hopkins," and "God bless you, dear" to the Sergeant and a passing turn, and we drove to our turning, and he thanked and blessed us for our company, and in our hall Katrine was so overcome that she sank on to the settle and said she'd leave her home for Pipson. I had gone for the letters at once. The post always intoxicates me; everything it throws on to the mat is a magic square or oblong which may alter your life. We were both humming with music, light and well-being, and in these states anything wonderful may be awaiting one. I pointed to the one letter for Katrine and was lost to the world in my own mail when she gave a little cry that brought me to earth in a second. I picked up the fallen sheet and said, "May I?"

"DEAR MISS CARNE,

"The committee has followed your work with attention for the two terms during which you have been a student, and has come to the conclusion that it is not justified in advising you to complete the course. . . ."

This was one of those bad moments which occasionally come to families.

I had so much to say that I struggled to select any bit of it and failed, as I usually do; all I managed was, "Shall I go down and see them, myself?" I can fight for other people. And in the end, as usual, Katrine and I went and told mother about it, and I left them alone. Mother has a knack. . . .

In my bedroom I walked about and fidgeted till two o'clock, addressing the committee in telling and acidulous phrases. It was money they were out for . . . if Katrine was so unsatisfactory a student it was their plain duty to have informed her after her first term. . . . I hesitate to designate their action as a plant, but how could they square their treatment of my sister with the undoubted fact that students patently more unsuitable than her were not only retained but promoted? . . . Boiling, muttering, I prowled. I wrote it all down, for the written statement invariably calms me.

How sorry and indignant and sympathetic Toddy would be when he heard! But Katrine wouldn't be in a state, for a few days yet, for us to tell him about it at lunch or dinner. . . .

Would Mildred play up? Would the kindly Brockley in her come up trumps? I rather thought so.

I stood in front of a photograph of Toddington leaving the Old Bailey, and said, "Oh, Toddy, we're in *such* a mess!" and then I cried, and then, in the odious way that these things intrude themselves, I began to dramatise the situation and to plan a story about it for *The Rattler*, and I wrote out the plot, crying all the time, and got into bed at three, and had no sleep till five o'clock.

In the morning there was a letter by my plate refusing my novel.

CHAPTER VI

IN the schoolroom, Agatha Martin was writing to her eldest sister in Cheltenham.

"DEAREST FLOSSIE,

"I have not heard from you for a week, so that makes seven days without a letter.

"I cannot tell you, tho' you should know, after all this time, how one looks to the post, when one is with new families.

"I think I am settling down very fairly well. Mrs. Carne is, I think, a v. nice woman, though a little bit weird! Anyway, she is v. nice to me, they all are. The two elder girls v. well-mannered, on the whole. They both do things. Katrine (eldest) is studying for the stage, but I think it may v. probably be only a hobby, tho' she is v. pretty in the brunette style, and speaks her parts loudly and clearly. Deirdre is a journalist, as I have told you (?), and really gets taken, and Mrs. Carne seems to let her go about to v. weird places alone. I don't pretend to understand the modern girl. Sheil, my little girl, is a sweet kiddy to look at, but a *v.* weird child. A kiddy who says whimsical things every now and again I could understand and cope with (do you remember Kenneth Barlow who said that 'King Henry died of a surfeit of *lampshades*,' and how heartily we laughed over it? He meant *lampreys*!!!) But Sheil isn't amusing a bit, that way; she talks in such a silly way about things and people, sometimes. It's perfectly harmless, of course, and I am sure I can get her out of it, in time, but one sometimes can't make out when she knows she is 'making up' and when she believes she is telling the truth. For instance, she told me yesterday that Crellie (their terrier) once thought he was the Pope, and had a procession to the Vatican, and he wore a cope, and just as the service was beginning, he was sick on the altar steps.

"But I shall watch all that. And the only scrap of foundation for the whole thing is that the dog is always vomiting because he will bathe so in the Serpentine, and swallows it. And even the elder girls go on about him, and sort of intone '*In Seculae Seculorum*' sometimes when they see him, and call out 'magnificats' whenever there is a Tom on the wall, and they say he 'talks' with a cockney accent, and sometimes meals are a perfect *Beldam* (do forgive! I mean Bedlam, of course) of cockney, and of what Crellie 'said.' It's so ridiculous, and not funny, as I said. I love a joke, but this is *v.* wearing. And the latest seems to be about—of all persons in the world—Mr. Justice Toddington; I fancy he was the Judge on the Poisoned Caramels case about three years ago? They are all silly about him, and talk in such a way that I can never make out how much is play and how much serious. They know him in private life, so I expect to meet him any day, now. He is certainly exceedingly generous, and I have often heard them talking amongst themselves of the presents he makes them on birthdays and at Xmas, so I await the next birthday with the greatest curiosity!!

"But my work with the child may be difficult; I shall have to be extra careful to be *commonplace*, and try to bring her to see that there is plenty of mirth in *everyday* things—more than in fanciful things which never could possibly happen.

"How is the Pater? And has the Bouverie Society a good summer programme? How *excellent* Canon Stepney was on 'The Gentle Art of Laughter,' last winter! I sent a line from his lecture to the *Morning Post* for 'The Trivet,' but with no result. I heard from Mabel, yesterday. Her old lady seems to be breaking up, poor thing, and Mabel is beginning to be a little anxious about the Future. Violet writes that she is getting her girls on capitally at hockey and that her school is to play Bradley this term."

Miss Martin put down her pen and stretched her hand and contemplated the schoolroom. Mabel and Flossie on the mantelpiece, Violet on a carved bracket. The men were in her bedroom. Captain Martin (retired) by her bedside, and Mr. Francis on the dressing-table. Miss Martin's chin trembled. Those photographs . . . she could see the studio in the avenue at which they had all attended when they realised that they must, as a home, disperse; knew her own portrait was represented in the two other bedrooms she would never see: in Bournemouth (Mabel), in Hampshire (Violet). Flossie's alone was dearly familiar, but the Pater must have a daughter at home. It was cheaper than a second servant. He would be lost without her. She knew his ways. The extra frame—Mr. Francis, was peculiar to Agatha, and Miss Martin began to dwell on him, once more. He had never actually proposed (men, somehow, didn't do that), but there had been, not quite an understanding, perhaps, but much mutual regard, and, on one side, a passion of admiration. But, of course, a junior curate's stipend . . . the Pater's pension. . . .

Mr. Francis: so unlike the humorous paper conception of a curate. Always a joke ("And where is Miss Betty? I begin to suspect she is all my eye!").

Manly. . . .

From the bedrooms a flight below came voices.

DEIRDRE'S: "What's Toddy doing now?"

MRS. CARNE'S: "Asleep. It's late. Hurry into bed, lamb."

DEIRDRE'S: "With one ivory claw against his little face!" (*Sounds of tooth-brushing*).

KATRINE'S: "What are his pyjamas like?"

MRS. CARNE'S: "Blue and white, from Swan and Edgar."

DEIRDRE'S: "Darling! Can you *see* Toddy getting his things there!"

MRS. CARNE'S: "I expect he gets them by the half-dozen from the place in St. James's Street where he bought the dressing-gown last summer that was too long for him, and he was so annoyed with us for offering to shorten it."

Miss Martin sighed.

CHAPTER VII

WE were to leave for Yorkshire three days after Katrine's letter came. Miss Martin was to have a fortnight in Cheltenham and then join us. We've told her about Katrine; what use trying to conceal it? I was honestly glad the Martin, at least, was going to be happy, and regardless of possible consequences, I sought her company. But the creature, cornered, simply isn't there. Oh well, I understand. Oh, how I understand!

I went into the schoolroom to try and outface the dismantled and trunkish atmosphere everywhere else, but it's no use. That atmosphere is all over the house.

Toddington is still on circuit, and I wonder what his wife's plans are? He's in Bristol, so one won't even see him before one leaves, and then he gets ten weeks vacation before the Michaelmas Term begins. Mother says he's sure to ring us up a lot, in Yorkshire, as he would if we were in America. He must have got a feminine streak in him, to be so understanding, but all the nicest men have, just as all the best women have a dash of masculine in their make-up. I hope Mildred has, too, but I never felt we really knew her, though we came nearer ever since she kicked her shoes off and said "whatever."

Katrine and I were sitting in the library the day before we left town, and I began to wonder if one might talk about everything, for she had gone about the house dreadfully bright for two days, now, and prompted the Martin to remark to me that she was taking it wonderfully well. . . .

I caught Katrine's eye.

"Hang it, K., that Dramatic School isn't the only pebble on the beach. You've had a lot of fun out of it, but it's an awful time-waster. There are shorter cuts than that."

"Such as?"

"The stage, fool!"

"Tah!"

"If you mean business, go out and get a job. It's done, you know."

"Oh my dear soul, don't talk that 'earn while learning' stuff to *me*."

"It would be a lark, K. Think of the frightful people you'd meet, and singing 'Bird of Love Fly Back' at auditions, and being told by an overdressed Hebrew in a hat two sizes too small that he'd 'let you know in a few days'! They all say that. It means you don't get the job

and he doesn't write to you," I urged. Katrine
brightened.

"I can't guarantee that you'll get kissed
much," I admitted, "and you'll almost certainly not get 'insulted' by the offer of a flat
and diamonds, because there's too much competition, so hardly anybody gets offered that
any more, and there's a perfect queue waiting
to be insulted, and in any case, most chorus
girls come from perfectly nice homes in South
Kensington and behave like nuns, these days.
But you'll be called Kid and Dear by the other
sort, and I once heard a producer telling a
troupe to 'dance it with debunnair.'"

"Hah!"

"I know. Of course the language is rather
awful, sometimes, but really it's mostly old
English, and Harrison Ainsworth is full of it.
Even Queen Mary said 'God's death!' when
Courtenay threw her over for Elizabeth. It's
awfully rum what you can get used to. I
remember when I first heard a girl say 'bloody'
I really felt bad about it—quite in the 'what is
youth coming to?' vein, but we say it all day
long ourselves now."

Katrine was beginning to look more natural,
so I drove the last nail home. "Keep young at
heart, dear gurl, and—who knows?—your little

lamp may illumine some Difficult Step for another."

Katrine began to join in, showering advice on herself. "Smile it off! The Cloud will pass away. Always refuse dishonourable offers with politeness, Pansy. Courtesy costs nothing."

But I saw that all this was only a flash in the pan, so, quite soon, I went up to the schoolroom again, dodging open bedroom doors in case somebody called out and wanted me to address labels, or haul at trunk straps, a job no woman ought to be asked to cope with. Even a holiday that is going to be a successful one should never be preceded by irritating and exhausting details. One should simply walk out of the house into a car, and be driven, coolly, to the station. And when one arrived, a maid would have unpacked. That's how it happens in the Toddingtons' house, and quite right too. The end of July certainly does search out the standing of a family, and our sort of departure is even apt to look all wrong, possibly because there are five of us, and all women. In the old days there was father, but we were living, then, in a ghastly house in Hampton Wick, and when I was a child and Sheil an infant, our departures to the seaside included a nurse in the cab and a bath on the roof, and that very nearly cancelled out father.

We certainly have two servants, but they
don't do their bit, and have Legs that have to
be Remembered, and Hearts which have to be
Considered, and I often groan for the Toddingtons' faithful cook, Grania, and the aloof but
efficient parlourmaid, Henderson. But of course
Toddy is a big man, and his progresses about the
country inevitably stately, and his adorable way
with all of us only serves to emphasise it.

And I sat in Sheil's chair and looked at a
supplement of *Cherry Ripe* on the wall, and said
for probably the fortieth time, "Oh, Toddy, I
wish you were my father!"

After all, the post is vacant, and it is mon-
strous that anything should stand in the way.
I'm sometimes certain that Toddy would like
it, too. I'm often afraid he's disappointed about
having no children, and the riddle of whether
Mildred "wouldn't" baffles me yet. I once
woke up in the middle of the night being
disappointed for Toddy.

He is going to Sandwich again, this year, for
part of his holiday, and I suppose the autumnal
end of it will be a series of house-parties,
probably in Scotland.

I do hope his hotel in Bristol is comfortable,
and that he has a private sitting-room. This
time last year he was on the south-western

circuit, and had to bundle off to Devonshire, and we think an old treasure of his age ought to be exempt, and just be in the Law Courts all the time. It's like throwing a leading lady away on tours.

... Or perhaps we could get made his wards? I'd rather love to be a ward, and it needn't be any trouble to Toddy. I suspect that Mildred might smell a rat, though, somewhere. I'm convinced she doesn't appreciate Toddy; she's too smart: one of those large, upholstered women who play a lot of Bridge and shop at Harrods (it is a definite type), and they've rather grown away from each other. And sometimes she says things that are clever and hurting and damnable, and Toddy goes away to his study and pines, and Henderson brings him in his tea there.

It's what a study ought to look like: one could do work in it and yet be happy. It has a coal fire and a gas one, too, for when he comes in a little damp from summer showers, and huge, rather ugly chairs that invite sleep, and one wall is books from floor to ceiling, though half of them are above the lay head, and under his desk is a fur-lined foot-muff. To give Mildred her due, she does see to his comforts.

I wonder what he's doing, now? Sometimes

the papers publish stingers he's delivered in court to counsel or witnesses, and we can all "hear" him saying them because he's just the same in London, and I seldom come away from his Court without some titbit for the family. He never jokes for effect, as old Horatio Sparrow used to; he is very silent and grim, and suddenly sweeps off his pince-nez and gives a dry remark or an awful snub, and they are always apposite or deserved and make me grin. Once, there was a thunderstorm, and he looked up at the glass roof and said, "I wish they'd stop that noise," and when everybody laughed, his face instantly became a mask, and he very slowly took the assurance out of a barrister, and when he'd reduced the poor creature to deferent speech-lessness, looked at him for a long time over his glasses, and then, very deliberately, went on making notes. We all long for a glimpse of that book of his. Sheil says she thinks he draws dragons in it and colours them in chalk after-wards with Nicholls, and Katrine once ventured that he was only putting down his washing.

When Sheil came in, I said, "Shall we be Toddy's wards?"

"Oh *yes*," beamed Sheil. "Does it mean dressing up?"

"'Fraid not."

"Then let's don't. Deiry, we saw a duck on the Round Pond to-day, and he had such a Millicent sort of face—kind of bright and helpful and silly."

I glanced at Miss Martin, but her face, for days now, has been a vague, happy blank. She is miles away, already. But I did the policeman act, for the look of the thing.

"Don't get whimsical on me, sweetheart. You'll be telling us all that the flowers talked to you, next."

The tactless little wretch roared with appreciation.

And then it was time for lunch, and we had one of those inexcusable scratch meals that servants always send in, if they dare, when a household is disorganised. And I sat there in absolute despair. As for mother, she spends the first week of any holiday recovering from the packing up, and was looking horribly white, and altogether the occasion was so appalling that afterwards I gave in, and told her about the publisher's letter. I'd tried to keep it to myself . . . it's somehow always been far more my business than Katrine's to shield her from trouble . . . but one has got one's breaking point. I can always forgive and understand it in other people, but never in myself. So I found myself saying, "Mother, the book's been turned down," and mother dropped a pile of clothes and held out her arms.

I wish one could cry as readily as some seem to be able to. After all, one is a woman. . . . I only know I can't, before people, however healing it would be.

A little later, mother took her cheek from mine and said, "Toddy's come from Bristol! It's Saturday, and he's got half to-day and all Sunday. *Isn't* he an old dear?"

I gasped, "Oh, Toddy, my pearl!" He had evidently got past the clumsy doubts of the servant, and had come upstairs alone. He said that he would stay with us until Sunday night, and that Mitchell would drive him back to Bristol, and that he had telephoned Henderson to get his room ready. He took my hands and said, "Dear Miss Deirdre, this is indeed a crushing blow. Believe me, I feel it every bit as much as you could."

Mother said, "You wrote to him, then?" and I answered, "Oh yes." I asked him if he'd told his wife, and he hemmed and hawed a bit, and plucked off his pince-nez and finally said no. And then he caught sight of the pile of cami-knickers on the bed and asked mother, "What

are these objects?" and mother said, "You'd
better not ask, Toddy. I might tell you," and
Toddy said, "Tscha! Obscene!" and mother
told him to "run along home now, and come
back to dinner," and he lectured her about the
use of the verb and said that, if desired, he
would *go*. And we told him not to be cross, and
he kissed us both and promised to "wait on" us
at seven-thirty.

Altogether, I went to bed strangely cheered.

CHAPTER VIII

MOTHER has always adored moors, and the wilder, the more windswept and (from my point of view) generally morbid the prospect, the better she enjoys it.

This type of place should only be gone to when you are very happy indeed. Otherwise it is too poignant, its unfair power over you of scarred rock, rusty ling and buffeting wind, too tremendous.

We stayed at a village five miles from Keighley, and almost from the first, as I had foreseen, everything went wrong. I think Katrine guessed, too.

The heather came right up to the exiguous back garden of the Inn, and it seemed to me that the general tone of life, there, was one of siege. The villagers know it, deep down, and that is why they have adopted their protective dourness; and that is also at the root of their famed hospitality. It's a gesture of defiance at the Unknown that crouches, and waits. The herding instinct that cattle know, in storms.

Sheil and I shared a room with an uneven

68

floor, and the wind banged round it so that sleep was impossible until one grew accustomed to it; and when it dropped, which it did, suddenly, like a voice which cracks on the top note of fury, the stillness pounded in one's ears. And then a fine, yellow sunlight, without warmth, bathed the moor.

Katrine and I went for long tramps. Sometimes we shouted to each other, but the sentences blew away in streamers over our shoulders. In the distance, we could occasionally sight mother, serene, at home, drinking it all in—owning it.

"Let's go our favourite walk," I would say to Katrine, with bitter sarcasm, and this led us for two miles to a village where there was a tiny "circulating library" at the back of the fancy goods.

Four miles for a book! We would bring back all we could manage at a time, but it was heavy work, and I thought, we shall exhaust it long before our time is up, at this rate. It certainly gave me an insight into the works of Mrs. Henry Wood and Miss Braddon that I had never expected to acquire.

The place was so blatantly bracing that it was odd one didn't feel the good of it. One was merely battered without anything to show for

it, or wetted through by the fine, whimpering
rain which would fall for half-days at a time.
Katrine wasn't looking well, but then trouble
always flies to our faces, and Sheil caught a bad
cold the first week and didn't seem to shake it
off as she usually does. Crellie revelled in every
moment, and scoured the country-side for live
meat. He had apparently unearthed a boon
companion, a bigger, rather rough dog. Sheil
had often seen them gambolling together, she
told us, and Crellie's friend is boisterous and
snarls a lot, and even the best game usually
hovered on the verge of a fight, and frequently
ended in one. We sometimes heard them at it
in the distance when we were at meals in the
parlour of the Inn, and asked the landlady if the
dog was hers, and she said she hadn't got one, and
that "Curly's" friend probably belonged down
at one of the miners' cottages. I knew them.
The mist hangs over them sometimes until mid-
day, long after it is clear everywhere else.

I had brought my novel with me in the faint,
hypocritic hope that I would find the spirit to
send it elsewhere. I kept it open, so that I
could suddenly read stray pages and try and
find out what ailed it. Mother used to go to
bed early, healthily tired, but Katrine and I,
when we were alone in the parlour, would sit

up late reading, or discussing the future, until the lamp often died right down.

"Isn't this being plain hell!" Katrine would mutter, night after night. "You've got your writing——"

"—only I can't do it. One can't do *anything* here but shake one's fist. And the people depress me."

"The red-haired boy was frightfully squiffed again, last night."

"Which one?"

"He comes into the bar. One can see him over the curtains, through our door. He's rather plain, with a white face, and talks a lot and looks as though he might be interesting. He doesn't seem to go down a bit, though, and is always telling stories that nobody listens to, so they might be worth hearing. If one ever succeeded in amusing these clouts with a story I should know it wasn't a good one," Katrine concluded venomously.

A sound came from overhead and she said, "Sheil's started a cough now, poor toad." So we abandoned the parlour and went to bed. Sheil was asleep, and I lit the candle and sauntered over to my manuscript and began turning the pages.

Publishers take too much licence. Let them

return the typescript, but not embellished with pencil notes. There were not many, but the principle remains the same.

"This is unworthy."

"Your thought, here, suffers confusion."

"Your intention is pure, but we all feel the inherent worthlessness of such a nature as you depict."

And

"Your Frenchman is, indeed, a laughable creature. *D'ailleurs* is wrongly inserted in this sentence. *You are the Frenchman*, and must suffer him to be acquainted with his Mother Tongue." I was excited with annoyance. It was awful that my book should have been read and chuckled at . . . I was so pleased and happy, writing it.

"*We* all feel——"

We, I suppose, were the publisher, his typist and his office boy. Something about the comments eluded me, and then it returned.

Of course! Term-end reports. There was a scholastic smack about the notes that used to permeate all our reports at school.

One has to wait until mid-day for the newspapers, which are sent from Keighley with the bread. We take in the *Mail* and the *Post*, and Katrine had just brought them in to mother, next day, and we were sharing the *Mail*, when

mother looked up and said, rather breath-
lessly, "Dion Saffyn is dead."

"No, oh no!" I cried, and then added,
idiotically, "The *real* Dion Saffyn?"

"I'm afraid so."

It was in both papers. The *Mail* gave him a
paragraph (*this well-known entertainer . . . concert
parties in Arcaly . . . a popular artist . . .*).

"How?" Katrine asked. She was rather
white. I think I was, too.

"'Heart failure following influenza.' We
mustn't tell Sheil. She was so fond of him."

"And Pauline, and Ennis . . ."

"I know . . . *poor* old Saffy. Well . . . he's
had a good innings."

Katrine and I got up and went out.

We didn't speak much as we flogged along.
There was nothing to say, and too much.
Katrine got the nearest to anything when she
stopped and faced me in the sheep-track we
were following, single file.

"It's . . . funny, isn't it, that we haven't the
right even . . . to send him flowers!"

"Or ring up the girls. . . ."

Part of our life was over. We both knew that
Saffy might come back to us, or might not. He
might have to, for Sheil's sake.

"How many years is it, now?"

I stopped again, to reckon.

"Over ten."

A singular thought struck me.

"And Sheil's never even seen him. Only photographs."

At the end of a fortnight Miss Martin joined us. She was, in her contained way, unsettled. The place, of course, didn't help her out, and her version of it was that it was "very wild." Her rendering of wrack was "quite weird," and as she became more de-Cheltenhamised, she also grew in unhappiness. She joined us on our walks, her neat feet and picked ankles decently navigating the scrambles, but she really preferred a trot up and down the high road in front of the Inn, while Sheil, swaddled in wraps, sniffed and coughed at her side.

After supper, Katrine said, "Let's table-turn." She said it, I know, out of contempt for the whole place, and the forced inaction and the one post a day, and no bath, telephone, geyser or Sunday papers. For we all regard table-turning as the kitchenmaid of the psychic world. It's too easy, too slavish to all of us, and tells far-fetched and clumsy lies, and altogether it's like twanging the banjo when you might be playing a viola.

Mother, always a little self-conscious with Miss Martin, asked her had she ever done any table-turning? And Miss Martin looked hesitant and bright, and was evidently being torn between her duties to her Maker and her employer, plus an illogical conviction that the whole thing was "great" rubbish. I very nearly said it all for her. Inevitably, rubbish and employers won, and we sat in a rough circle.

"*Agatha.*"

"Why, that's me," squeaked Miss Martin.

"Don't take your hands off, Miss Martin. It means it wants you to ask it questions."

"Oh . . . dear." Miss Martin fluttered and tittered. "What—what do you want?"

"*Where have you been?*"

"Chah-Cheltenham."

And then, in the maddeningly inconsequent way they always do, the table rapped out "*red hair.*"

"No, oh no. Mine is brown." Katrine kicked me under the table and I said, "You'll have to dye it, Miss Martin," and mother said, "S'sh."

"*Crellie and Keeper. Not pleased.*"

"Crellie and—there isn't a keeper here. Lor! I hope he hasn't run a sheep," said Katrine.

"*Crellie bit Keeper.*"

"I bet he didn't, did you, my fattest?" I protested, slapping the sleeping Crellie's stout stomach. Then, suddenly,

"*Sheil come.*"

"She can't. She's in bed," explained mother.

"*Go back.*"

"Where to?"

"*Go back.*"

"Please explain," mother asked, with that matter-of-course courtesy which she would play impartially upon servants or demons.

"*Remember Maria.*"

"Who's that?"

"*Remember Maria. Remember Elizabeth.*"

"Is it 'Maria' or 'Elizabeth' speaking?"

Pause. "*No.*"

"*And remember Anne.*"

"Dear! . . . all the queens of England!" chirruped Miss Martin. "Where is 'Anne?'"

"*Not here. You would say dead. Not here. Further. Sea.*"

"Which sea?" I asked, for Miss Martin was, like Doctor Watson, "a little nettled at this want of confidence."

Pause. "*North.*"

"'Anne dead in the North Sea,'" I commented.

"*Not in. By.*"

"This is rather slow," complained Katrine. But the table was at it again.

"*We will come.*"

"What, all of you?" smiled mother.

"*The two who came before.*"

"That means Queen Mary and Queen Elizabeth," said Miss Martin. "Anne was so much later."

"*Not Queens. C-H-A-R-L-O-T-T-E and A-N-N-E.*"

"When will you come?" enquired mother hastily.

"*Not yet. Not free. Shall we see you?*"

Then, as we returned no answer,

"*K. promise.*"

Katrine yawned and said, "All right."

"*D. promise.*"

"Very well," I said.

"*R. promise.*"

But mother is too old a hand to be caught that way, and I could see that she removed her hand for a second, and made the sign of the cross.

If one could say of a table that it expressed contempt in sound, that is the word I should select for the performance of ours. At this gesture, it was for all the world like the rappings of overbearing knuckles.

"*Anglican. No Popery!*"

Mother smiled to herself, and Miss Martin went "hoo!" right up in her head. We silenced the hail of raps with our promises, the table rocked into a corner and we shuffled with it.

"*Sheil—go—back—in—time.*"

After that it would say nothing.

Miss Martin said it was perfectly weird.

As I moved about the bedroom, Sheil stirred in her sleep, and gave a husky little crow.

I stood a minute in the middle of the floor, and slinging my dressing-gown round me, opened the door. Mother's room was at the end of the passage.

Outside, she was coming towards me.

"Well . . . what about it?"

"I agree with you," I answered.

"There's nothing serious the matter with her, but at the same time——"

"I know."

We packed the following day.

And so, Katrine and I were able to be at Dion Saffyn's funeral. We hid in a back pew, and when those with a right to be present had laid their wreaths and driven away, we came forward and put our flowers with the rest.

In the church, I could recognise nobody, but

Katrine pulled my cuff and whispered, "That's Pauline—the fair girl up in front. She's changed a bit, but it's Pauline. I remember her face. . . ." As we left the churchyard, I said, "K., I do hope you don't want hymns for your funeral. They make one feel——"

"Not much! Have what you like, if I do go off first. I'd like some of German's *Nell Gwynne* dances."

"Why can't they let one have a medley of all the music one's ever liked? After all, it's more 'us' than *The Day Thou Gavest* or anything of that kind."

"I know. I love all sorts of things: *Gathering Peascods*, and *Vanity of Vanities*, and *I'm One of the Ruins Cromwell Knocked About a Bit*, and if one asked for them, they'd say one was irreverent. Aren't people incredible? What are we going to do now?"

"Cinéma? That ought to kill or cure."

"Couldn't stick it."

"Tea?"

"Couldn't down a thing."

"Better be on our own."

"Right you are."

I walked and walked, confused with the way things were going and by the fact that I was in London in August. Somehow, the sight of town

was rather improper, like seeing your grandmother in her combinations. You knew she
wore them, but the shock was none the less.
London in August was one of the sights automatically kept from you, like major operations,
and yet I have always suspicioned I could love
it at forbidden times. One misses so much by
slavery to dates and clocks. How many Lon-
doners have seen the vegetables unpacked in
Covent Garden? Or the day dawn in Kensington Gardens, or breakfasted at Greenwich and
gone back by steamer? And if it comes to that,
how many of us have seen the country in
October, with wet apples thumping overnight
on to the ground? Poor little Pauline and
Ennis. What a break-up! I wonder what they
do? Saffy really has got a London office, and
when I am in Leicester Square, I pass it and
look up at the windows.

Sheil is better already, but she and mother
must go away again and finish up the business.
Saffy's death would throw Pauline out of a
job, I had said to mother, and then I remembered that probably she had never been in it
. . . she may even be married. . . .

Oh well, there's always work.

CHAPTER IX

I WAS returning from Kensington Gardens, the aquatic Crellie, wringing, beaming, and full of pond-water and tiddlers, lumbering on ahead. I adore the autumn and all its smells, and the schoolroom would soon be dark enough to be lit for tea. This October was doing and being all the right things: warm as a June night, and full of subdued colour.

When I got home, mother leaned over the banisters and said, "Mr. Binton's been ringing you up. He wants you to telephone him."

It probably meant nine hundred words on "Should Widows Re-Marry?" ("Have you seen the *Express* this morning, Miss Carne? There's a paragraph on page 7, column 5. I'll read it to you.") A journalist is always supposed to be able to give the casting vote on these questions, and the fact that she is neither wife, widow, nor what-not, is worried about by nobody.

"Hullo?"

"That you, Miss Carne? Didn't you tell me a while ago that you'd like to meet Todding-

ton . . .? Well, there's a bazaar next week at
the Albert Hall for a Legal charity, and Lady
Toddington is taking a stall. That any good
to you?"

I stammered, "You're an angel," and heard
Binton giggling. The moment I had rung off
the whole thing flew to my knees, but I got it
told to the family, somehow. "And Binton said
'Lady Toddington,' mother, so Toddy must be
a knight."

"Bless him!" said mother.

We didn't know that judges automatically
became knights. It's a perquisite of office, like
the bowls of dripping the cook sells to the rag-
and-bone man. And to think my own familiar
Binton had known it all these years. . . .

"Oh Toddy," I exclaimed, "you will be
pleased to see me, *won't* you?"

"I shall be delighted, my dear," answered
Sir Herbert. "I cannot hope to be with you
and Mildred before five, but I trust you will let
me give you tea."

"Are you going to have to spend an awful
lot, my darling?" asked Sheil.

"Well . . . you know . . . these affairs . . . I
think a five-pound note should cause me to
emerge without a stain on my character."

"Well, I think that's handsome," I said.

"It is expected," answered Toddy, with that note of finality he always uses when we have overstepped the mark.

"It's in aid of the Browbeaten Barristers!" Sheil gasped. Sheil, that week, was my safety-valve. At lunch she would shrill, "It's only three days now before Deir' meets Toddy!"

Miss Martin, of course, didn't seem in the least excit_d . . . her *sotto voce* comments seemed to convey an attitude of well-what-about-it? that had the usual sedative effect.

"But—she's going to *meet* him!" glared Sheil.

"Yes, dear. There's nothing so very unusual in that, is there?"

At the eleventh second, mother managed, "It's rather an occasion, you know," to which, Miss Martin, patently at a loss, responded, "Oh, of course," then more happily, "these huge bazaars are very fashionable affairs sometimes, aren't they?"

"He mayn't be there at all," I cut in, robustly facing the situation. But this was treachery, and Sheil cried out, "He *told* you he would. He gave Mildred a cheque for some Lalique to give her stall kick. You said so, mother!"

"Do you know Lalique, Miss Martin?" Mother smiled with her eyes at Sheil. "It's a rather wonderful sort of glass . . . no two designs alike . . . Frenchman . . . factory pieces . . . less costly . . . Sloane Street. . . ."

(Miss Martin thought it sounded very quaint).

And, as if life wasn't doing enough for one, it shot a letter on to the mat at tea-time that made all four of us do our special dance—the famous "Pas de Quatre," to the hummed music of Meyer Lutz. We only know one of the original steps from theatrical memoirs, but for the time we are all old Gaiety stars, and mother sometimes joins in too, very lightly and neatly.

I knew the letter was going to be an interesting one because the envelope was square and thin, and the writing unfamiliar. Probably one of my readers, who got me out of the telephone book. We are always howling over their poems, and I picture the writers in their shirt sleeves, sitting on Sundays in the kitchen, breathing heavily over their penny bottle of ink. The unintelligentsia seem to be prolific letter-writers, and I am long used to being asked to meet cycle-makers outside the Coliseum, and to walk out with widower plumbers who write to me on their trade paper, with pictures of lavatory basins on it. Mother once bought a basin from one of my flames, but got no reduction on the price.

The letter was written quite badly enough to qualify for the plumbing stakes. I looked first at the signature. It was from Pipson.

"MY DEAR MISS CARNE,

"I beleive you mentioned that your sister was hopeing to go on the stage, and I am wondering if I havent something that might suit her. The fact is that I'm booked for revue for six months and if your sister would consider joining the chorus I havent a doubt my reccommendation would get it. It would be tour most of the time and salary low, but you never know. Now my dear Miss Carne you and sister must overlook anything in my suggestion but I know how difficult it is for a lady to get a start. If I may say so, I could put her up to tips as to digs, etc. Above is my p.a.

"With compliments to all

"Yours very sincerely

"F. PIPSON."

I tore upstairs to the drawing-room where tea was going on, and when Katrine and mother had got the gist of Pipson's letter, we shouted up the next flight, "Sheil! Pas de Quatre!" Sounds of protest, and a flurry of small, delighted female. Forming in line we kicked our fill. When we'd finished and were having fourth cups of tea, Sheil asked what the dance was for, this time, and she sat by mother and ate cakes that were slightly forbidden, and Crellie stole a macaroon and didn't get smacked because of Pipson's letter. And when Miss Martin was discovered in the doorway with resigned complaint in her eye, Crellie belched at her, and mother began to laugh and said, "I'm so—sorry, ha ha!—Miss Martin. Yes, go now, darling, oh, ha, ha, har!"

"The stately an' memorable progress of this 'owly man to the Vatican," began Katrine, "was only slightly marred by a passing indisposition——"

"What *is* a 'p.a.'?" said mother.

"Permanent address," answered Katrine.

"My darling, how truly awful! There'll be two plaster lions on the gate-posts and a stone cauliflower on the lawn with a red-hot geranium in it that never gets watered. P.a. . . . it's subtly worse than a 'villa residence.'" Then with a look at me I knew. "Is Pipson all right?" Her look brushed aside Katrine's protests and testimonials.

I just nodded. Her face relaxed instantly.

"We'll go for a perch this evening, after dinner," rejoiced Katrine, and I think we all began to look forward to it. We love walking at night: one feels so light and fresh, and passing faces are shadowed and can't tire one, or sadden, or set one thinking. And we go hatless, with walking-sticks, and wear what we like, which is restful, and find ourselves in strange streets and squares, and sometimes they abruptly conduct one to eminent localities, as in a dream, and I once found myself outside Buckingham Palace in my dressing slippers. We call these walks "gutter-perchings" and they are wonderful, if you are happy.

"And now I suppose La Martin is offended," remembered mother.

"She made a rather heavenly face when Crellie went into liquidation," said Katrine.

Dinner was a priceless affair, with mother at the top of her form. She had just helped herself to a wing of chicken and suddenly began to imitate her French mistress at the school where she was educated, and then she burst quite extempore into a parody of the poetry they were made to learn—all optimistic and no base thoughts of men entertained.

"(Attention, mes enfants)!
  'C'était un beau jour d'Avril,
  Les fleuves ruisselaient,
  Les oiseaux—piroquaient,

Et—sur le gazon tendre et vert
Les belles têtes émaillées des fleurs apparaissaient.'

(Une marque de désordre!)" Then, to herself, "That's really *dam'* good!"

"If it's Victor Hugo it's much better than him," I agreed. We know by repute all of mother's ex-mistresses, and imitate them nearly as well as she does, and once when we were reading our old exam. papers we found two of ours and three of mother's, and she said, "May 1874 . . . would those be yours or mine?"

We set out at nine-thirty.

"I suppose Mildred took all her stuff down in the car yesterday," mother said.

"Yes. She had a tea the other day to show the Lalique, and sold quite a lot in advance."

"We'd better ask her to dinner afterwards, and tell her she must come just as she is, and can go when she likes."

"Better not," answered mother, "she'll be dead tired and will want to go straight home."

"I wonder if Nicholls will be there?"

"I'm certain he won't. He couldn't afford the prices."

"Oh, *poor* lamb!"

"Toddy can tell him all about it," consoled mother, "I expect he'll take him out to lunch."

Henry Nicholls is a dear, and Toddy is

becoming increasingly fond of and dependent upon him. He has left him £250 in his Will. Nicholls does a hundred jobs for Toddy that don't come within his duties, and seldom rushes off to snatch his own lunch before he has seen to it that Toddy is served with what he enjoys, and last summer when Toddy gave a lunch-party in his private room at the Law Courts and Mildred came to hostess it, Nicholls must have had only about ten minutes to himself, as he volunteer'd to shepherd us all and wait by us in the hall until we were all assembled when Toddy could come down the stairs to lead us up without loss of time and being gaped at. And Toddy said, "Are all my ladies here?" and mother, who overheard, said, "Yes, all waiting for you to crack the snail for them," for we are always trying to wean him from alluding to us in the rooster manner. It's purely old-world, but we find it dreadfully hen-coopy.

When we had walked another half-mile mother said, "Well—to-morrow you'll see Mildred. I'm longing to know what she's really like."

"But, darling, come too—and buy some Lalique!"

"Not much! This is your show. But you must tell me every mortal thing."

"She'll probably be a crone in a bugled dolman," said Katrine, coming out of her Pipson trance.

"Oh no," answered mother and I. After that we talked about revue.

That was a wonderful day. One never guesses in the morning when one gets up that some days are going to be like that.

CHAPTER X

THE Albert Hall bazaar was no sort of a job, professionally speaking, and one not a bit in my line. With that fact I tried to steady my nerves all through lunch, while Sheil stared at me with passionate concentration. To her, I knew, I had already taken on the quality of dream. I was merging into the saga, and she, fascinated, bewildered, was watching me fade. . . .

I didn't feel any too real, myself, and Katrine and mother had caught it a little, as well, and we were all rather silent.

On that occasion, Miss Martin was our safety-valve: our responses to her remarks came briskly. One heard them being admirably apposite.

When I looked back, mother, as I knew, would be at the drawing-room window, watching me down the street. She called out, "My love to Mildred!" At my feet fell a bunch of violets tied with cotton. The schoolroom window framed Sheil, her russet wig starting.

Her shriek, "For darling Toddy," was half drowned by a passing motor.

Inside the hall I was pestered in the usual manner by women who seem to think that a hideous cushion is pretty if it is sold for charity. I suppose my trouble is that I haven't got "Press" written all over me, or a clever way with nuisances. Somebody loomed up and I said, "Is Mildred here?" and then I heard what I'd done and felt rather ill, and stammered, "I mean Lady Toddington."

I found myself being led in the direction of her stall.

"That is Lady Toddington. In blue."

She was very much as I had expected, only smarter and a trifle younger. Her hair, instead of being dyed, as we had all arranged, was anybody's brown rapidly growing grey. And she was business-like, which put me out of action, for a bit. . . .

I handed over my Press card. Somebody was explaining me. And then, I found myself let in for one of those hopeless conversations which are inevitable where one party has a lot to do and the other nothing. But that was only the stupid, obvious difficulty. The main trouble lay in the fact that I came to Lady Toddington aware: primed with a thousand delicate, secret knowledges and intuitions, whereas to her I was, I suppose, merely so much cubic girl, so to

speak. I felt at once at an everlasting disadvan-
tage and as though I was taking her friendliness
under false pretences. A sort of Judas at the
keyhole.

How could I tell her that I had lunched with
her and helped her dress her stall, yesterday
afternoon, and that Toddy had come in after
the Courts rose and given us both a cocktail?
How convey the two years I had spoken to them
both every day of my life? How blurt her own
life to her, her daily round of dressmaker,
telephone, at homes, and tiffs with Toddy. How
describe to her her own secret difficulties: that
she is privily aware that she is not his mental
equal? That in the past there have been days
when she would almost have welcomed his
tangible infidelity as being a thing she could
roundly, capably decide about, and no brains
needed? That she has long ceased to love and
notice him?

And what would she make of that £250 left
in Toddy's Will to Nicholls? Or of Toddy's
mistrust of Saffy as a suitable friend for us?

And what would she say to the mushroom
story, in which her husband got a "naughty"
fit and refused one morning to go to the Law
Courts and hibernated in a burrow, and, for
more complete protection against discovery

and interruption, fixed a mushroom to his wig?

That sort of tale we recognise as fantastic. We know how to be reasonable. . . .

Meanwhile, there was the spadework of the situation to get through, and I wondered how long it would actually take to bring her up to the point at which I had arrived long since, so that we could all start level.

One must curb impatience and be, if possible, careful. For the time, one must be ludicrously formal—as though one said "How do you do" to mother. I am rather good at that kind of thing. It's a horrid bore, because it involves a lot of doing of things you dislike, tactical planning, personal adaptation and looking ahead.

And thus, by dint of effacing myself behind her stall, wrapping awkward parcels in scanty paper, and fetching Lady Toddington a cup of slopped bazaar tea, and generally behaving like a lackey, I did that which I had set myself.

She "took a fancy" to me, asked me what paper I represented; and at that point I had to do another job and become slightly vulgar, as talking of one's achievements always seems to me to be.

She said, "It's wonderful what all you girls

are doing now" in that comfortable sort of
voice which non-combatants are able to use.
And she called it "gurls," but then, of course,
I had known she would. . . .

Towards the end of the afternoon, while she
was counting up the wages of sin, I succeeded
in saying, "Isn't Sir Herbert going to look
in?"

"No. He's going on to a dress rehearsal."

At this, I struggled with an insane impulse to
exclaim, "Why wasn't I told of it?" or "He
never said so."

Toddy at a rehearsal? A *dress* rehearsal?
M'm . . . the Garrick Club . . . that might account for it. In my confusion I hardly realised
the disappointment. But the idea of Toddy,
sitting sternly among a crowd of actresses
nervous to roping point and patting their curls
all over him, was rather sweet. The family
would adore it.

I answered at random, "I love dress rehearsals," and indeed I have been to many. I prefer
life in its shirt sleeves. And then the absolutely
incredible thing happened.

She asked me home to dinner.

Luckily, I go very white when in the least
tired or excited, and this seemed to smite some
maternal chord in Lady Toddington in spite of

the lack of "s." or "d." as *Who's Who* tersely describes offspring.

I sat within two feet of the brass warming-pan, and for the first time saw the street from the right side of the window-boxes, and felt like Alice on the mantelpiece.

We had iced consommé, salmon mayonnaise, vanilla soufflet and a pineapple, so that Toddy was evidently properly looked after, as far as creature comforts go.

(*To give Mildred her due, she does see to his comforts.* Which of us had said that?)

During the meal I put some of my cards on the table: told her about my visits to the Law Courts, which she took placidly, saying she thought they were dull and the ventilation "shocking," and just as I was going to put down another card a small dog trotted in and she hailed the creature as "my Mingy," and I thought, "That dog is born to be my curse," for he (or she) was the sort of dog that actresses bring to rehearsals.

I said, "Is he your dog, or Sir Herbert's?" and she answered, "Mine, isn't he, a boy!" and to me, "Sir Herbert hates him."

I thought, "We'll soon get you out of speaking like that, my woman!"

"Sir Herbert." To me! To anybody, if it came to that. Oh. So Toddy hates him. He would, of course. And I glanced at her face for concealed resentments and found none; only a business-like acceptance. Well, they have been married for forty-six years. . . .

And then she garnered us all into the drawing-room and I said I admired it, which was the truth, and that I was enjoying my coffee, which was a lie. It was a good blend but servant-made. The room's proportions are charming, long and high-ceiling'd, one of those Georgian rooms still left, thank God and beauty, in London squares. And the night was blue and very calm and warm.

There was a crystal chandelier ringed with electric candles whose light fell on a piano, the lid of which was covered with silver frames and sundry other sins against the Holy Ghost, and Lady Toddington asked me if I played, and unfortunately I do, so that meant fifteen minutes reft from eternity while I deliberately soothed her with Co-Optimism and the more melodious refrains from current revues. I took a chance on the strong probability of the Moonlight Sonata being dismissed by her as Very Nice, and soon had her humming and tapping by a sentimental syncopation I had

composed myself as parody of the popular
trend.

> It was something in the air
> That made her do it.
> Something in the air. . . .

I rambled, with the full allowance of Jazz
breaks.

And then Toddy came in.

Half an hour later, Lady Toddington was
saying, "You must come to see me again."
Always a crucial sort of remark, as it may mean
anything or nothing. But she added, "Come
to my next At Home. Thursday."

Sir Herbert opened the front door for me. He
couldn't know, of course, how many times he
had escorted me to the top of the road, and
suddenly I was aware of a faint sweetness, and
it was Sheil's violets begging to be remembered.
I surrendered, appalled, and gave them to
him. I said, "These are from Sheil, my sister.
She is eleven and a great admirer of yours."
(Faugh!)

For a second he played true. His face
relaxed its formality which I, of all people in
the world, had been responsible for.

"How very dear and charming of her. My
most grateful thanks."

I have no recollection but one of getting home. That was that I drew my case from my bag and was taking out a cigarette, when the mental mist lifted, and I saw the policeman on point duty looking at me in an interested manner.

I had expected mother and Katrine to fall upon me like vultures, but the essential improbability of the evening smote them to momentary silence. So might the family of Joan, ruminating over the evening meal of bread-soup and *crêpes*, greet her return after the angelic interview. Poor Sheil had long been asleep. I was all for waking her and serving her the cream of the news, but mother said no, which helped to bring us down to earth.

"She'll never forgive us," I warned. That was probably true, but the real reason was that I was in an agony of impatience myself. Sheil has often betrayed me into inveighing with her against the common sense of "the grown-ups." She knows, too, so well! that there are some things one must have at once, and that to wait for them, even five minutes, spoils everything.

I once bought mother a large pear, and, burning for her pleasure, rushed home to present it. She happened to be telephoning, and said, "Just a minute, darling," and left me there, deflated, thwarted, my pleasure gone.

And when I told Sheil, years later, she said promptly, "I should have thrown it out of the window."

Sheil and I nearly always love the same things. This was at the root of her blind, advance adoption of Toddy in the weeks that followed the Jury summons. Sheil is not very used to seeing her familiars and playfellows in real life, and was enchanted at the extra bonus when allowed to pay a visit to the Law Courts with the governess. She sat, it seems, drinking him in, and horrified Miss Chisholm, the predecessor of Miss Martin, by unwrapping one of my photographs of his lordship in Court and frankly comparing it with the aloof, seated figure. Going home she said, "He is *very* pretty, and yawns like tiny jam tarts." And Miss Chisholm, who had seen an old, frail man in pince-nez, austerely putting people in their place, told her not to talk nonsense. Why must children have governesses? They trample, in their business-women's shoes, upon a thousand delicate flowers a year, and sow such boulders in exchange. The Chisholm was a thoroughly good sort, and a perfectly deafening bore. After that, Sheil refused to admit that Toddy's name was Herbert, and christened him Austen Charles. It was, she said, the right name for him with a face like that. And I agree. Mother said she hoped Sheil wouldn't grow up to write novels of the type she calls "lofty leg-pulls."

And even that, said Miss Chisholm, was not all. When he whom she described as "the Judge" had concluded his six minutes' summing up Sheil had applauded heartily. That was my fault for forgetting to tell her that it wasn't the same as a theatre. Sheil, if I know her, sensed the drama of it, just as I do, and she wanted, the dear! to support the old firm, but it was no good. Miss Chisholm was troubled at being made conspicuous, and sensibly dreading a repetition of that agony, she suggested that mother should "speak" to Sheil.

And when we three were alone and Miss Chisholm had retired to remove her business-like shoes, mother obliged. She hoisted Sheil on to her lap, gave me her spare hand and said, "Did Toddy say anything, or did he just look at you over his glasses? The old pet!"

"I think he did that, but afterwards I expect he and Nicholls rushed away to grin in Austen's room," answered Sheil.

Katrine had come downstairs, too, to hear. I began to tell them, snatching about at random in a hurry, for I don't talk or explain well, and never did.

"Toddy is very like himself. I saw the top of his head for the first time. It's only the tiniest bit bald and he looked very silvery and sweet and younger than in his gown, and he didn't stay very long and talked about the rehearsal——"

"*Which* one?" implored poor mother.

"(Oh, one he'd been to. I'll tell you about that, later). And he seemed quite knowledge-able about the stage and I can't see yet whether his teeth are false——"

"(They must be, at his age)"

"(I don't know. Look at Grandpa). Well, then he was rather funny about the bazaar, and said, 'Aren't they horrible?' and he was much more kind of *all there* than we make him."

"Well, you couldn't really expect the poor old dear to be quite the antick creature we say he is——"

What I meant was that Toddy, from a negative, had developed into a print, and inevitably during our half-hour together he had spoken out of character, and shown himself to be possessed of his own personality as against the semi-fit that we had allotted him. I had expected this, but the little shocks were no less

real. . . . Telling it all took a long time, and even
then the real business only began when we
dispersed to our bedrooms. Said mother from
hers, in the Toddington voice, "Deirdre!"

"Yes, Toddy darling?"

"I was so pleased to see you this evening."

"Bless you, my pet! Has Mildred gone to
bed yet?"

"My wife?"

"Hah!"

"Yes, I believe so."

"Why didn't you come to the bazaar,
Toddy?"

"How kind you are to be so informal."

"Hah!"

"I was at a rehearsal. Um . . . yes. . . ."

"Did they crowd round you, and make a
fuss of you?"

"I received every courtesy from those ladies."

"Oh, come off it, Toddy!"

"What do you mean? Who are you speaking
to?"

Katrine chipped in. "I expect the star sat
on his knee."

"Who is this person? Introduce me."

Toddy is never at his happiest with Katrine.
For months we have introduced them to each
other laboriously every day. Whenever she

annoys him he makes this request. Katrine loves baiting him, and he comes to mother and Sheil and me for redress and sympathy.

By midnight it transpired that Toddy had set the entire company right upon a point of law, had been given a box for the first night, in which two chairs were to be sacred to mother and myself—we to dine first with the Toddingtons and then "go on" in their car, and that he had been himself driven home by the leading man with whom he had made an engagement to play billiards on the following evening at the Garrick Club.

After all, why not? Toddington must have done exactly that sort of thing dozens of times. The worst of it is that, when the evening comes and one isn't dressing and the car isn't outside, one is so disappointed that it is tiring.

But the looking forward to the evening is lovely. . . .

Mother's final words were, "And the Lalique! Did she have a lot?"

"Not a hap'orth! It was suède bags, and little disgust-boxes of olive wood."

CHAPTER XI

AGATHA MARTIN was shut into her bedroom.
The schoolroom was pleasant enough, but she had
often read that governesses were not expected
to have a human side, and in any case the Carne
girls, particularly Deirdre, used her pupil's room
to a degree which was surely unusual.

Mabel's old lady was dying—she took up
Flossie's letter. There was a rumour that Mr.
Francis was to be transferred to another curacy.

Miss Martin turned yet again to his photograph. Between the two exhibits she unhappily
pondered. Then, from the inner flap of her
writing-case, she drew three closely, neatly
written sheets. They were signed Arthur M.
Francis, and in phrases well-expressed, if a little
stilted, he offered her marriage. They would be
definitely poor, but he ventured to think that as
neither Agatha nor himself was of extravagant
habits, as their outlook on life was essentially
settled, as neither was one of our Bright Young
People, he thought that a fire and a pipe for him,
and a fire and some fancywork or a book for
her when the day's long trick was over. . . .

Miss Martin smiled a little at the Bright

Young People touch and the Masefield reference. They were typical of the man. Then she dwelt again upon the sincere love he had for her, the admiration of her pluck in becoming a part of strange families . . . the words swam before her eyes. What need to read on? She knew the letter by heart. She had written it herself. It was nearing the end of October, and so there was always the schoolroom fire in case of emergency.

Goodness really knew where Carne vagaries might move Agatha next summer, not that they could take her much further from Cheltenham than that appalling Yorkshire village. Such uncomfortable rooms, and the natives so terribly weird and unmannerly. Their sittingroom so close to the public bar, and their privacy not always respected, with that redhaired boy staring in over the curtains whenever he wished. A little more, and Agatha would have mentioned it to Mrs. Carne. She had suspected once or twice that he was not sober.

It was, perhaps, the contrast of having travelled to it all fresh from home. Arthur had called round twice, and they had had one of their glorious afternoons under the mulberry, with the Pater in good spirits and Flossie more like a mother to him than a daughter. But already there were changes. Agatha's desire for re-

incorporation had, it seemed, meant little adjust-
ments. Already she (and presumably Violet and
Mabel) was counted out of the domestic reckon-
ing. In the future, they were to be beloved
visitors . . . Agatha Martin looked involuntarily
and with a dreadful clarity into the future.

There was a postal order to send to Mabel.
She would not have saved much of her salary
. . . that winter coat . . . Arthur would be certain to drop in to say good-bye, if the rumour
was true. On the other side of the writing-case
were several letters from him; newsy, semi-
affectionate, semi-fraternal.

What a year!

Unfamiliar railway stations, one's trunk
marooned on the platform. And all over the
country, Violet and Mabel on platforms, too,
wondering what their bedrooms were like?
For that was, now, what mattered most . . .
and Mabel, soon to be out of a post, for which
she must hope as she must dread.

Agatha wondered how it had all come about?
It was, she supposed, inevitable, since finances
were the Pater's concern, and if his arrange-
ments for his family miscarried, the universe
was to blame for a display of bad taste. What
a mercy she herself was a Newnham woman!
And that, before Cheltenham suspicion could

have been awakened. The dates tallied, beautifully . . . quite three years before the Pater had
to retrench . . . Arthur had called her Our
Blue-stocking . . . and threatened to appear
from her wardrobe, suddenly, at one of the
cocoas, and get her sent down in disgrace ("I
want to hear what you girls really do talk about,
only I'm afraid of being horribly shocked").
They had often stood joking on the pavement
during the morning shopping, Mr. Francis
leaning on his bicycle.

For a long time she dwelt upon the idea of
writing to him again. He was a friend of the
family . . . it was a bother that Sheil said so
few quotable things . . . but professionally
speaking, Miss Martin believed she had cause
for congratulation in general directions. There
was, for instance, a sensible diminution in the
nonsense-talk about that Dion Saffyn at luncheon, and his probably imaginary and in any
case unremarkable daughters. It was only when
they all returned so suddenly from Yorkshire
that she, catching sight of the paragraph about
his funeral, had condoled with Katrine about
it and discovered—Miss Martin was overcome
by a backwash of indignation—that the Carnes
didn't know him, even slightly. Katrine had
said so, quite coolly, very quietly reducing

Agatha to bewildered Buts—, then with an authority she had never assumed before, "Miss Martin, we have all agreed that Sheil mustn't be told, if you don't mind trying to remember," she walked out of the schoolroom.

After that, ready, she assured herself, for anything, Agatha was quite prepared for the Toddingtons to go by the board as well, but her calculations were thrown out once more, and Lady Toddington called, and remained to tea . . . Miss Martin had been present. She considered that Lady Toddington was probably one of the most respectable friends the Carnes possessed. A society woman. But when—Miss Martin compressed her lips—it came to persons like Mr. Pipson, she thought Mrs. Carne was' going altogether too far even for Katrine's sake.

He had come to tea a week ago—driven up in an immense car, and had been treated altogether as an equal by his hostess and her daughters. Agatha had made the terrible mistake of liking him, in spite of his accent and grammar. He had been most attentive and polite, and by his abstention from bad language or calls for beer, had given her no clue whatsoever as to who or what he was. He said to her, for all to hear, "Ah, I often wish I'd had more education. If you'll believe me, Miss

Martin, I couldn't write till I was fourteen, and
as for spelling—well!" and she, assuming he
was some business magnate of such long
standing that his beginnings were purged,
opened her mouth to expound her theories to a
sympathetic ear, when Mrs. Carne said, "I
can't spell, either, Mr. Pipson," and Sheil,
bright-eyed, called out, "*I* won't spell if you
can't!" and had evidently taken one of her
terrible fancies to the little man, and that meant
goodness really knows what, for Agatha to cope
with and disperse. And she dragged him
upstairs to see the toy theatre, and he examined
it and said, "You'll get the L.C.C. down on
you in the twinkling of a ton of bricks, Miss
Sheil," which remark, for the usual baffling
reason, delighted the child, for she exclaimed,
"Now I *really* adore you!" and Mr. Pipson
said, "Then we'll be married on the Tuesday,
if it falls early in the week, and I'm not laid
up with one of my attacks of synopsis of the
scenario." And then they had walked round
the little garden, and he told Mrs. Carne what
to do for green-fly and how to deal with wire-
worms ("My gardener's a good man but that
old-fashioned you wouldn't hardly believe.
Now, what *you* want to do, Mrs. Carne——").
And he showed Sheil some dance steps, and the

child was enraptured, and they cut capers all
over the borders, and Mrs. Carne laughed until
she cried. But as he was shaking hands he
looked at Katrine and said, "In a fortnight we
shall be in Bradford. Eh, Braaadford!" then,
to his hostess, with a sudden seriousness, "You
can trust me to watch out for Miss Carne as if
she was my own, Mrs. Carne." And Mrs.
Carne said, "I know I can," and he put his arm
round Sheil and said, "God bless you, dear,
pleased to have met you, Miss Martin."

Later, Agatha delicately approached the
subject of the departed guest. It had called for
tact, of course, but the elder girls, she had to
admit, were seldom touchy.

"A charming man, but—would one say he
was *quite* a gentleman?"

"Pipson? A gentleman?" answered Deirdre,
"he's a low comedian, Miss Martin. He's
Freddie Pipson."

And it was then that Agatha had begun to
see that his good manners were merely bo-
hemianism, helped out by the courtesy of
herself and the family. The Carnes should
have warned her, but they were an incalculable
family. Kind, in many ways kinder than any
of her previous families, but, somehow, having
the effect of making one want, as never before,

to have a long chat with Flossie, or to set out on a good walk with Violet and Mabel. . . .

The latest Carne joke, it appeared, was to say, "Pleased to meet you," whenever they passed each other on the stairs, and to do what they described as "pipsonising" at meal-times. Deirdre would say, "If you'll pardon me, Mrs. Carne, you're commencing to cut the beef wrongly, if you know what I mean," and Katrine would reply, "If I'm not robbing *you*, may I ask you to pass the cruet?" then both together would enquire, "Is your tea as you like it?" And even Sheil would call out, "Don't spill it, Miss Carne; if I may pass the remark, whatever are you doing?"

Agatha had actually stopped all this. Sheil was admittedly her province, and her own possibly impulsive rebuke had nominally been addressed to the child. But she rather thought the others had taken the hint. . . .

"Well, really, Sheil, I quite thought Mr. Pipson was a friend of yours, but one wouldn't say so to hear you making fun of him." Silence had fallen round the table. Sheil flushed angrily, and began an incoherent sentence.

"I wasn't making fun of him. When—when —when——" then, tiresomely, Deirdre finished her meaning for her, a way she had. . . .

"When one is really fond of people, you know, Miss Martin, it's sometimes the greatest compliment one can pay them."

Agatha, at a loss, remembered that she had replied, "Then I shall look forward to the day when you all begin to imitate *me*," and Mrs. Carne offered her more beef. But after that there was no more Mr. Pipson. "It may take time," thought Miss Martin, "but in the end I think one's influence will be felt." It was all quite harmless, but it was beyond doubt the result of friendships with impossibles. It was lucky for the Carnes that they had known the Toddingtons for some years, or they might have scared them away, but Agatha supposed they were accustomed to it all, by now, though Lady Toddington had certainly seemed rather formal with them, for a friendship of such long standing. Now Agatha came to think of it, she had kissed nobody, on leaving—except Sheil, of whom she had said, "I can't help it, she's such a little pet, aren't you, Baby?"

Agatha, praising Lady Toddington later to the elder girls, had delicately regretted the public compliment, and Katrine said, "Ah, but you see, Miss Martin, she's got no s. no d.," and Agatha had hinted that she understood that Judges made very high incomes, and

Katrine and Deirdre had burst into great noisy
shouts of laughter.

Voices outside on the landing: Sheil's shrill
"Pass the preserves, please," and Deirdre's,
"Believe me, laddie, I was a riot at Hartlepool.
The Guv'nor offered me ten pounds to play
Harmlett, but I said, 'I won't touch it under
fifteen, and that's m'last word.'"

Katrine cut in: "The Bard, laddie, the Bard
needs playing. But pass me off with fit-ups and
ask me to double in brass and I'm thrown away,
dear boy, thrown away!"

Steps on the stairs, and Mrs. Carne's voice:
"Trrr-a! mes enfants! Ah, Trotty, ça marche,
hein? Amuses-toi bien, ma mignonne!"

"Oh shut up, Ironface!"

"Hé? Shot op? Mais, qu'est-ce que c'est,
ce 'shot op'?"

"Go away. It's pure affectation, Ironie—
and you who came from a suburban village
shop!"

Mrs. Carne said, "Now you *have* done it! She's
flown back to Isidore." She added, "Ahem!
Let's be talking, said Mrs. Kenwigs."

Miss Martin began to cry. She remembered
to muffle her face, because Deirdre had caught
her, once before.

CHAPTER XII

REALLY knowing the Toddingtons was, I should think, rather like marriage: sometimes it was disappointing and at others it exceeded expectation. The disappointments were affairs of the cook not being faithful and dour and Scotch, and called Grania, but an angular Cockney whose name was Bessie; and of the parlourmaid answering to the name of Ethel, who, so far from being tossy and called Henderson, is eminently approachable and seems really fond of both the Toddingtons, with a slight list to larboard in favour of Sir Herbert. But female servants always prefer the master of the house. I don't read Freud, but I suspect that he would explain why, in gross and in detail—particularly in the former.

And then the rooms in the London house . . . Toddy's study, for instance. The fireplace was, from our point of view, on the wrong side of the room, and his armchair on the right of the gas-stove instead of the left, while his bedroom was even on the incorrect side of the second-floor landing. Otherwise, it was very much as we had planned it.

When Lady Toddington first took me "over" the house, after her at home, I noted, of course, plenty of familiar things: an overcoat and a walking-stick and umbrella of Toddy's, of which I have had photographs for eighteen months on my own mantelpiece, and one of his hideous little jam-pot collars on his dressing-table, and I knew all about that, too. It figures in all his portraits (except when he golfs at Sandwich, and then his neckwear is winged).

I remembered his college trophies, and found one or two, in study and dining-room, and I knew that in one of his cupboards hung his hunting-coat. I had never, so to speak, seen it in the flesh, but I knew when he had worn it last, and where.

Following in the wake of his wife I walked as though treading on glass. Liable to be confounded at every turn, my remarks were probably going to be shattering in one direction or another. Actually, I only made two false steps that afternoon. One for each plane. We had stepped on to familiar ground after much that was strange when she led me into the dining-room and gave me a cocktail, and this episode, and my relief at rejoining the current, made me incautious. Mildred absently looked out of the window and suddenly seemed to see her own window-boxes and said, "They're half dead already. I'll never have geraniums any more. Last summer we had lobelias."

"No. Calceolarias," I answered, putting down my glass. Luckily she failed to "hear between the lines," and only fastened on to the flower, which she said she was sick of.

The second occasion was infinitely more serious. It was also bad luck, as I might have easily come out with something traceable by her to a tangible source, such as news items or *Who's Who*, had her conversational lead happened to veer in another direction.

She is, obviously, one of those open-hearted women who are apt to play expansiveness upon friend and acquaintance alike, and this again caught me off my guard. At the moment, I forgot that it was a manner rather than an accurate gauge of intimacy, and for that moment we were in the current again: we were Deirdre and Lady Mildred having cocktails, with Henderson shortly due to swim along the hall and take away the tray.

It must have been past seven, and she glanced at her wrist-watch and said, "Lord! I must run and dress. We've got a crush on to-night." Then, in her sociable way, behind which I sensed that she meant it, "My dear, don't marry a brainy man unless you're brainy too. Must keep one's end up all the time."

"*That*'s not what he likes best," I answered.

"Eh?"

I fell upon the subject. "Toddy's rather easy to misunderstand. We used to, until we got the hang of him. That austere business, you know . . . but he loves best to sit and smoke and be chaffed, and lots of books, and a dog to take out——"

"*Chaffed?* Herbert?"

"Yes. He knows his manner frightens people, and inside him he wants people who'll get past all that. . . ."

"Well——!"

"There are so few people, Lady Mildred, who have the time or enthusiasm to—to dig for one, don't you find it so?" I was actually, in the excitement of the moment, putting in a word for Toddy; was trying to break down the smart, Harrods-and-Pekingese side of Mildred that we all believed existed, superimposed on the kindly Brockley that we all agreed was there. We know now that the dressy, Harrods side of her had never seriously existed at all—it was one of our bad guesses. Inevitably one makes a few.

She put her glass down on the tray. "My dear girl, how long have you known my husband?"

That was an easy one. "I don't know him."

"But——?"

"I've met him once, for half an hour, on the bazaar evening," I answered, speaking like a witness in the police court.

"Oh—I see." She seemed to be engaged in some mental wrestling match.

"And, by the way, I must have seemed abominably impertinent. I'm afraid we all call him 'Toddy,' at home, and I'm awfully sorry but we call you 'Lady Mildred.'"

"Toddy" . . . she toyed with it. "He'd bite your nose off if you ever called him it."

"I'll sell it," I answered, smiling at her.

"Nothing doing, my dear. I should catch it too."

"I believe he'd adore it. He'd pretend not to for ages, but he'd go away and shake all over— you know his way, and then come back and make one of his long-lip faces at you . . . Good Lord! I'd better go!" I ended, appalled.

"Have another? No? I'm going to. Well, you seem to have thought it all out!"

"I'm dreadfully sorry, and I *am* going!"

"Don't, unless you must. You know, I like you. I don't know many young girls, I wish I did. I can't make you out, but I ought to be used to that b'now, with people . . . you know,

I'm the sort that ought to have a hat trimmed with ostrich tips and a feather boa, instead of model gowns and shingles and trying to live up to everybody."

"You're a *dear*," I said.

Somehow, one had never arranged to get really fond of Mildred, before . . . I wondered what difference it was going to make?

"I'm glad. Nice to be liked, ain't it? Even if it's only reflected glory. Bless you, I'm used to that."

"It isn't that, a bit."

"Come up and let's hunt out a photo of Herbert for you. He hates me saying 'photo,' by the way. Can't imagine why."

"Does he object to 'whatever' too, on the same principle?" I chuckled.

"Probably. But what *is* the principle? Now, here we are." She opened a bureau and slid a sheaf of Toddy's portraits on to the sofa, and began to offer me various prints. I vetted the lot in no time, though I pored over the studio photographs.

"Oh yes, that one was taken outside the Old Bailey . . . yes . . . the Barkston Gardens case . . . on the golf-links at Sandwich . . . thank you awfully, but I've got that one . . . yes, I remember this . . . that's not one of my favourites, besides, I've got it." She looked at me in a bovine amaze, and we suddenly began to giggle.

"If you'd just put the one or two aside you *don't* happen——" said Lady Toddington, and howled. I pointed with a trembling finger to three studio portraits.

"Tha—tha—those . . . I can't imagine how I came to overlook them, ha, ha, ha!"

"I shall begin to suspect you of I really don't know what," announced my hostess.

"*I* do," I answered, blowing my nose, "but you'd be wrong, worse luck," and we roared once more.

Lady Toddington began to remove her rings. "No, but have you really got a crush on him?"

"Well, yes and no," I said, wiping my eyes. "It's not quite as simple as that, you know."

"But—look at his age. It seems so un-natural."

She'd be sure to say that. Even the nicest women are apt to have Mrs. Peachum minds. They would be horrified if one told them what they really meant.

"Don't you think," I answered, picking my words, "that it's rather—bad luck on people to have to give up being loved because they're old?"

"Of course I do! But, a girl of your age. . . ."

"I'm afraid that dog won't bark, Lady Toddington. Look at Sheil. She adores him. You remember her?"

"The little thing!" ... Lady Toddington went off at a tangent. "I like your family."

"Good chaps, aren't they?"

"You're all happy together. One can see that. So few mothers and daughters seem to hit it off these days. It almost makes up for not having a girl of one's own . . . to think of all the fights one's escaped! Well, go on, tell me more."

"Well, Katrine—my other sister, is going into a revue and my father is dead and we've got a governess who cries into soup."

"Whatever for?"

"Hah! I don't mean she really does, but the poor toad is homesick, and she's got three of the usual sisters and a retrenching father in Cheltenham. And she keeps a stiff upper lip. And you can't imagine, Lady Mil—Lady Toddington, how people who keep that sort of thing get at one!"

She was listening like a child, sitting by me on the floor, her feet stuck straight out in front of her. "You see, I follow all her worries." I saw she made nothing of this.

"Yes. I remember her. Came down for tea,

didn't she? Poor wretches . . . you've got a rather specially sympathetic nature, haven't you?"

"Not really, because half the time I don't want to be."

Lady Toddington laughed and lit a cigarette. "Well, go on. Tell me more about Herbert!"

There was a knock and she cried, "My Lord! and I haven't begun to do anything! Come in."

Toddy stood in the doorway, and I tried, for the mass of photographs on my lap, to scramble to my feet.

"Well, Herbert—you remember Miss Carne?"

Miss Carne, clasping six of his heads to her bosom, shook hands with difficulty.

"How do you do. Are you having a sale of jumble, Mildred?"

"I know I'm not dressed and I know dinner is nearly ready and that the dressing-gong went ages ago."

His eye—I saw, for I was watching for it— twinkled at his wife's instant exposure of his rebuke, but she had already begun to go slightly to pieces, it seemed to me.

"It's my fault, Sir Herbert," I said. "I'm one of those door-steppers who never seem to go."

"But, please! And let me relieve you of all those encumbrances."

"You'd better not, Herbert. Those are pictures of the one slip I made in my girlhood."

"What do you mean?" He regarded her over his glasses so exactly as he does in Court that I laughed. Lady Toddington glanced at me. I am almost sure she thought I was going to be embarrassed and was ready, if so, to say something else which would put her wrong with him, but the answer I looked made her remark instead, "It's all right, my dear. It's Miss Carne's boy-friend," and I shuffled the prints together, somehow, and she looked up at Toddy and said, as a baby might plead with its nurse, "Herb', let's don't go out this evening. Can't we all stay and have a nice cosy time at home?"

He looked down at her, considering. "That sounds very charming, but it's the Slingsbys, if you remember. But can't Miss Carne stop to dinner, in any case? We needn't leave until nine-thirty."

"Well, that's an idea, too!"

Dinner was a nerve-racking affair for me. There was our Toddy within touch, and it was Mildred who kept us going.

She—for a course or two I haggled over the impression—was pleased I was there? And then, with the entrée, it came.

She was showing me off to him, like a mother. And I wanted to play up, but was handicapped

by the outrageousness of having to be the little
stranger to Toddy. And Lady Toddington, by
this time, knew just enough to enjoy the whole
business, and began, metaphorically, to dig me
in the ribs, and treat her husband and myself
like a newly married couple. If she'd had a bag
of confetti I swear she would have thrown it.
. . . and Toddy went on making one face after
the other that I knew, and being charming, and
it took me all I knew to keep upsides with either
of them.

One had got to get through to him sooner or
later, so I said, "I like your Associate, Sir
Herbert. He's got an interesting face."

"Mathewson? Yes. He's a very, very nice
fellow. I should be quite lost without him. He
told me once that he would have studied for
the Bar, only—money, you know. . . ."

Well, that was being all right . . . though
that part of it hadn't occurred to us.

"She adores the Law Courts," said Lady
Toddington, getting ready for another dig.

His face broke into its fine network of lines.
"It's a fascinating place, isn't it? And offering
scope these days for you ladies." I laughed in-
wardly and answered, "But the present lot of
women barristers will never make a living.
Their children may."

"I'm afraid that's true."

"Then, you're in favour of them?"

"Why not? The last word, you know!" and the old wretch glanced at me with his sub-acid brown eye. "I must admit, though, that I think, perhaps, the Chancery Division offers more suitable——"

"Ah. You mean rude exhibits handed round on a plate," I said. And at that he shook all over.

"Since you insist——"

"I believe you'd like to limit the ladies—God bless 'em—to droning about bressemers and hereditaments—by the way, what *is* a hereditament?"

"It's usually a waste of a good half-hour," responded Sir Herbert. "But, are you *interested* in them?"

"Adore them! The last time I dropped in, you said hereditament five times, and I thought it a gorgeous word. I love words."

"So do I."

And then we began, *via* his cases, to talk about murder, and he seemed pleased because I remembered that Seddon lived at 60 Tollington Park and Crippen's number in Hilldrop Crescent. From murders we inevitably worked on to the flood of books on the subject, of which I had read many, and from these to books in general. And from that moment Mildred began to fade out. One felt her personality withdrawing itself, and though I threw her one lifeline after another, it was no real use. And Toddy wouldn't help me. It was early days to expect it, but I was definitely cross with him, for all that. Engrossed, peremptory, he danced me off to his study to show me some first editions and I wasn't at my best with them, because of Mildred upstairs, feeling out of it. But before long the book-spell told, and we were swapping prejudices and worships.

"Whenever I happen to be alone for a meal, my book is *Vanity Fair*, and the parts I pick out to re-read are lunchy and dinnery. There's a smear of tomato sauce over Becky casting the Dixonary into the garden, and gravy on, 'And eh, Amelia my dear, I've brought in a pine for tiffin.'"

He adjusted his pince-nez. "Ah. I've got chutney on, 'When I stepped into the car'ge afther me mar'ge,' and tobacco burns right through the spontaneous combustion business."

"*Bleak House?* Can't get through it."

"You must try again. As a matter of fact, I once discussed that episode with a doctor, and he says it is, medically speaking, impossible. I adduced the haystack, which ignites of its own fermenting poisons, but he said that while breath remains in the body that form of death is automatically debarred. But it's a tremendous piece of writing, for all that." He selected a book from an upper shelf. "Are the Brontës beyond your interest?"

"Only Anne, and honestly, Sir Herbert, I think she's a perfectly crashing ass."

He gave me a wintry smile. "I know what you mean. The Brontë family has been, like Switzerland, too much stamped over, and virtues have been discovered in all their work which I, personally, won't admit it always possessed. But what a family! Even if they'd never written a line, what a story! Isn't it artistically complete that there isn't a quotable line recorded of Anne? Wasn't there a sort of fate which ordained that she, of all the family, should be buried away from home, dying, meek, futile, on that Scarborough sofa . . . and Branwell, drugged and drunk, dying, erect, in his best suit, out of bravado? 'My nerves! my nerves!' . . . I always wonder where that poor boy got his red hair from. It didn't seem to break out in any of the sisters."

"You think they were degenerates?"

"No more than I believe the lady who published a book trying to persuade us that Emily was spiritually hermaphroditic. The Brontës were, to me, the perfectly logical result of their environment, parentage and diet! . . . You've seen the museum?"

"No. We were in Yorkshire in the summer, but we never thought of going over to Haworth. We were too busy being miserable."

I looked at him, unreasonably hoping this would strike some chord, but then I remembered that Toddy had supervened wonderfully little, that fortnight, and as there was no telephone at the Inn he couldn't ring us up daily. We like to be exact.

"Miserable? Dear me. I am so sorry. I was at Sandwich."

"Yes. After the Bristol Assizes," I answered mechanically.

"Yes. I was really enchanted by the parsonage. Emily's desk as she had left it, with her housekeeping books . . . and that flower group on the wall over which Charlotte stippled her eyes away . . . and the pencil marks in the upper room recording their heights—the wall-paper had to be removed before those were found. Why one is so fascinated I can't imagine. It's such a little time ago, and yet, one is compelled to enchantment . . . when I was a barrister, I used to walk all over London finding addresses where Dickens' characters lived, and I shall never forget the moment when I came down Kingsgate Street, High Holborn and found the bird fancier's that Mrs. Gamp lodged over."

"How heavenly! Do go on going on!"

And he did; delicately pacing, sweeping off his pince-nez, tapping with frail little claws on covers, until the door opened and Mildred, who was now much more Lady Toddington, came in, a daunting figure in her hard, sparkling gown.

"Well, you book-worms! It's past the half-hour, Herbert." His face set, but it wasn't at her entrance, though I guessed she believed it to be, but at the epithet. Mildred, of course, isn't a clever woman, but she can strike for her own. She was summing me up; offsetting me against previous experience. "*I don't know many young girls.*" She thought that handicapped her. And then there was my three-years-old unfair advantage. . . .

I wanted, badly, to go to her—it seemed so natural—and put my arm through hers. I wanted to say, "Isn't Toddy looking a dear!" I wanted to tell them that mother sent her love and that they weren't to forget they were having supper with us on Sunday—sure of the instant response to which I was so used: "*Good-night, dear child. That will be charming.*"

But there I stood, at a loss, and watched Lady Toddington.

"The car is at the door, my lady."

She turned and followed the maid. I gave my hand to Sir Herbert and then Toddy said, "You must come and see her again, if you will. She would enjoy having something young about the place."

"I wonder?"

He looked at me as he does at an over-confident barrister.

"But I know." And then he gave me one of his lay smiles. I said, "You know, I've had a very wonderful evening." I'm glad I was able to lash myself into telling him that, and while he was folding his scarf and shrugging into his coat, I went to his wife in the hall, uncertain as to whom I should find there, and her first remark gave me no clue.

"Well, how's the idol?"

"The idol's a great treasure," I answered, "do you think it would ever come to see us?"

"Ask him. You seem to have made a hit with him. He says I read nothing but Edgar Wallace. Is that considered to be very bad?" She asked as she might have consulted with her milliner about the state of the fashions.

"I'll tell you one," I said, "he reads detective

stories himself. I saw three on the bottom shelf."

Lady Toddington laughed aloud and became suddenly Mildred. "Well I never! I'll hold that over his head in future."

I hadn't told her that the books in question were masterstrokes of their kind in which sleuthery was subordinated to style; I was counting on her being the type that would classify *The Two Magics* of Henry James as a ghost story. In any case Toddy must really try not to be a literary snob. I think that Mildred had taken the Edgar Wallace remark absolutely literally. It would be very characteristic.

She turned and put a huge envelope into my hand. "Don't forget your young man." She had brought it down herself. Perhaps I looked what I felt, for she put her hand for a second upon my shoulder. "Come and see him again soon. I"—she seemed to pause for a phrase, and then, I think, altered it—"I think he'd like it."

"And you, too?"

"Me? Oh, I daresay you'll find me putting down a saucer of milk for the cat! We'll give you a lift, of course."

So I sat in the familiar car that I didn't know was theirs, or hired, and the man who might have been Mitchell drove us.

I couldn't expect much sleep, that night, of course. I amused myself with turning over my albums of published work, and by dipping into my novel. I found that four years ago I had written three articles berating Mr. Justice Toddington for sundry things he had said in Court. Evidently Binton had suggested the subjects. Heavens! How I had got home on Toddy! I compared him with my pet aversion, St. Paul, and said that it was a pity that his biased private opinions should be aired in public. The affair appeared to be about the presence of women at murder trials. Mother heard me cackling, and came in in her dressing-gown. As she was leaving, she said, "By the way, aren't I ever to be allowed to read your book?"

"Oh mercy, darling! It's all over advice and remarks from the last beast I sent it to. If you'll give me time to rub 'em out . . . I remember which pages they were on."

She agreed instantly, kissed me and left me. I hunted for an eraser and turned up the pages. The pencilled comments weren't there.

Then I sat down and thought.

CHAPTER XIII

KATRINE is rehearsing in a rather attractive pub in Maiden Lane; it is mid-Victorian and seasoned with beer smells and there is sawdust on the floor, and when you've walked through all that, upstairs is a large room with a piano so dreadful that it is funny, and girls dressed in jumpers and knickers, and some of them practise in bathing kit and look very boyish and gay. The piano has one note which is dumb, and I always wait for it not to function, and guess when it ought to be doing so. It is A above middle C, and I never knew how important A was until the accompanist got started.

> I'm going (blank)
> To dreamy Hono (blank) lu!

Katrine and Sheil and I always sing "blank" now instead of the word or syllable when we practise the ensembles at home; and we did last Sunday, in church. We hardly ever go, because we believe in such a lot of things that aren't in the official list, but we wanted to pray for the success of the revue, and however modern or sceptic or advanced one may be, there is something about a church more likely to make wishes come true than anywhere else.

Two years ago I went to St. Bartholomew's to beg St. Rahere that Toddy mightn't die on circuit before I saw him again, and that his sheets mightn't be damp in his lodgings, and when father was ill I happened to be passing a Baptist Chapel and went in, and although I shall never know about the sheets, because Sir Herbert won't remember, father certainly became better, temporarily. I'm sure God likes small attentions, and I'm going to be nicer to him in future because of Toddy and Mildred, and Katrine thinks she will be, too, because of Freddie Pipson. So we sang

> Jesu, lov (blank) of my soul
> Let me to (blank) bosom fly.

and we both think God would adore that piano, as we do. Katrine doesn't know it yet, but she's in for a hot time in the provincial dressing-rooms. I hadn't been at the rehearsal five minutes before I picked out the company cats. I've never had much to do with them, but I've met more of them than Katrine has, and the type is rather prevalent and almost unmistakable. They are usually horse-faced blondes

with rodent teeth, who tell all the dirtiest
stories and generally have a grubby little pull
with the management—poor brutes, and are
always the first to go to pieces in a crisis. Pipson
told me that in the air-raids that sort of girl used
to lose her head entirely, and after saying God
and Christ steadily upstairs, dropped down and
prayed all over the stage when the bombs began
to fall.

We didn't see much of Pipson, of course. He
is such a great man that he rehearses in theatres
between the performances, with the principals.
He's got Katrine two wonderful lines to speak.
One is, "I've never been so insulted in the
whole of my life!" which remark comes into
every revue I've ever seen, and the other,
"Well girls, come on, the bathing's fine this
morning!" and we practise saying it in all the
most frightful ways there are. Katrine wants
to speak it in a Cockney accent, but mother and
I are in favour of "Wehl gehls, come on, the
beything's faine this morning!" and mother
once put on my béret and flung her evening
cloak over one shoulder and whipped a walking-
stick out of the folds, made a pass at Katrine,
and said it like Hamlet, pacing with a Reper-
tory stalk. But Katrine, thinking of the producer, said, "You want to soften that, dear,

it's altogether too strong." Mother sheathed her stick and declared, "It would be awful from the front, quite awful."

Katrine is picking up the dances quite nicely and we practise them in the garden to the joy of the cook and the incredulity of the Colonel next door, who creeps into his bathroom to watch us, and gleams at us through his monocle, and seems completely astonied, like the man in the Bible. Katrine was very nervous when she first saw him sternly watching us, and missed a step, but the garden is the best and most unencumbered place to rehearse in, and our movements are perfectly decent, so we have invented a place in the scheme for the Colonel, to account for his being there, and we pretend he is a masher left over from the Empire promenade who is trying to seduce Katrine, and that his gleam is one of unbridled desire, and when we'd settled that, Katrine was much more at her ease, and the rehearsals went with a swing.

We took Miss Martin down one afternoon to watch, because we felt it would be good for her general education, and she said "But" all the time she was steering round the barrels, and was rather stunned at the bare legs being directed by a man. I told her the truth: that the girls danced in their skin to save money on washing and darning tights, and that seemed to reassure her, economy being unassailably respectable. But for all that she sat against the wall expecting to be insulted, and appeared to be rather at a loss when nobody attempted to, and shrank when the girls came near her to rest, and talk, and examine the heels of their shoes, and went "hoo!" when one of the cats said, "Honest, kid, that's the second pair I've trod over in a week with these B—— rehearsals." Some of the girls say worse things than that, and I have warned Katrine not to tell mother because she mustn't be worried, and that she may have to say them herself on tour for peace and quiet, but that they aren't for family use. Katrine is already depressed by the language alone.

Miss Martin took it absolutely sitting because she didn't understand, and hoo'd solely as a tribute to the bad grammar going about. It has already leaked out that Katrine knows Pipson, and most of the girls assume that she is what they call his "friend," and have more or less divided, as a result, into two camps already, in which one side is awed envy and the other suppressed spite. We did tell mother about that because we thought she'd love it, and she did.

Sheil has begged to see one rehearsal, but I won't let mother allow her. The girls are nice, good creatures, with a few exceptions, and they would love her in that stridently demonstrative maternal way that the chorus does, but they are not for Sheil.

Katrine leaves us much sooner than we expected, as some dim managerial caprice has decided that final rehearsals are to take place in Bradford, where they open. Pipson has found her lodgings near his hotel, and walked round the question of fleas and bugs so delicately that we had to say them for him, which relieved him a lot, though he still calls the latter "what's-her-names," but he has known Katrine's rooms for years—long before he arrived at his present status, and though they will take nearly two-thirds of her salary he has advised her to engage them. Katrine would really have an easier time all round if she went into retreat in a convent, and far more chances of acquiring merit. She is too excited to feel leaving home, but she will be disappointed at being out of the fun on Hallowe'en. We have missed keeping it for years, since we left Hampton Wick, where we had parties on every imaginable anniversary, and having no proper garden now has made a difference, especially in the matter of

guys on the fifth, which were what we called a
spécialité de la maison, and famous all over the
village for their size and drama.

But this year, Sheil is old enough to join in too
and stay up late, at least, that is the official
excuse. Actually, I am pining for an illuminated
gourd-head with a jagged grin, and for the
black cats and witches on the table, and I
wanted to see if the young man in Miss Martin's
bedroom would crop up in the looking-glass
rite, and how she would cope with him if he
did. Being a thoroughly good woman, her
mind is probably not very clean, so I expect she
would look self-conscious, and think any woman
awful who didn't look the same way when
eligible males were offered her by the spirits,
who, I must admit, are apt to be rather heavy-
handed in their ideas of humour. I often
wonder if Miss Martin wants to be asked about
him, and I would ask like anything if it would
please her, though it would be terrible if she
wanted to be all-girls-together with me about
him, and I sometimes think there is an all-
girls-together side of her, if one could get down
to it. Katrine can't imagine why I am interested in what she calls the Martin's Rogues'
Gallery of portraits. She doesn't see that, with
people like Miss Martin, photographs take the

place of speech and give the outsider clues to
their lives. But then, Katrine can't imagine
what it must be like to be suppressed in any sort
of way, whereas I can. She fell in love with our
fishmonger when she was eleven, and made a
hero of him, and one morning she happened to
go into the shop when he was rating the
cashier for a muddled order, and she came home
quite pallid and said she had now got to the
age when all desire shall cease, which was
the last verse she had learnt, and mother
would have shrieked, except for hurting her
feelings.

Sometimes I look forward to that time,
myself, as love goes on for ever, and the sex
part is only an interlude, and, except for making
babies, doesn't really matter anything like as
much as people pretend. It is merely expedient,
while love has no fish to fry, which gives one
persons in one's life like Saffy and Toddy.

Katrine was so miserable at the idea of our
having a Hallowe'en party without her that we
promised we would give it up, and mother
suggested one on the first of November, as it is
All Souls' Eve, which didn't seem to us to be a
legitimate excuse for pumpkins, so we gave up
that idea too.

I wonder, if I were dead and allowed to

return once a year, whether I should like best to look in at windows I knew and see the living having fun and playing games, or whether I should feel less forgotten if they were sitting there being sad about me? All Souls' Eve should never have been put into November, because of the little chilly doubts in the hearts of the dead. They should have been allowed to come to us in high summer, when the air is still, and smelling of hot grass and sweet peas, and the moon is large and bland.

Father came back, once, but only once, and very naturally, so as not to frighten us. He was sitting all the evening in the library and was wearing one of his old lounge suits I had forgotten, but remembered at once because of the ink-stain on the sleeve that the cleaner couldn't get out. It's upstairs in a cupboard still. He looked up, very kind and pleased to see us when we took it in turns to peep in at the door, and we brought him our best toys and put them where he could enjoy them, and mother put us into our new party dresses for him to see, and told us to tell him everything we were doing, but not to mind if he didn't answer.

We know now that what Miss Martin would call "ghosts" can speak to one if they want to. Why father only came to see us once, I don't

know, but I expect that he knows we are always
here, if wanted.

Katrine's last days with us are passing, and
yet they can't seem to strike through to me,
because of the Toddingtons. I told her so, and
she understood at once. Lady Toddington has
made her return invitation, and when It was
imminent I was afraid. Once more the mon-
strous social occasion must be gone through—
even for Sheil, with whom Austen Charles has
long been a familiar, and if any hitch occurred,
one couldn't guess what would happen. We
can't afford another Saffyn death. . . .

I believe Sheil is suspicious about Saffy. We
have, at last, re-established him (he came to
lunch last week, rather suddenly), but during
that time of silence, after Yorkshire, I wonder?
I rather think children sense death as cats and
dogs do family departure.

That was partly why it was so important that
Toddy should take to Sheil. He must love her
for two . . . and at last, we had assembled the
conditions; Mildred, mother, Sheil and me at
the Toddingtons' house, with Toddy expected
home any minute. All as it had been a hundred
times before . . . with myself in the strange *rôle*
of guide. Literally, anything might happen.

All I could reckon on in advance was the known attraction of Lady Toddington for Sheil.

One of the difficulties is that Mildred has always tended to be the pawn in our game. Her creation was of necessity a more vague affair than Toddy's. She formed piecemeal, and I think it possible that if we hadn't known she existed we might never have created her at all. But we played fair. It took a year to get her into definite shape, and Sheil will have remembered that, and our early struggles with her hostess's personality; would remember that in Skye she herself had put Lady Toddington's age at eighty-four. Even Lady Toddington's tea with us hadn't been much help in materialising her, since, for the time, we were transformed into handers of cake to a visitor—our own familiar Mildred!

And so, we had filed in after mother into the Toddington drawing-room. Sheil, in her elf-green frock, sat on a gilt chair, her little paws decorously folded, her eyes upon the door in a shameless waiting for Toddy that, mercifully, only we could interpret. It was the face seen in boxes before the entrance of the leading man. Mother, of course, was being social and brittle and what Katrine and I call Martinesque, and I handed Lady Toddington's cups with my mind a chaos. It only occurred to me on our way home that the obvious thing would have been to have put that work on to Sheil.

"Let me see, you have another girl, haven't you?" said Lady Toddington.

Sheil started. Inevitable, these jars. I couldn't protect her against them. She has heard Toddy distantly squabbling with Katrine so often ("Who is this lady? Introduce me, if you please"), and revelled in the way Katrine riles him, and I knew that everything poor Mildred said was liable to shatter something. Sheil will have to go through it. It's the price of reality. Only, she is so young. . . .

And reasonably soon, there was Toddy's step on the stairs. He went the round of us, and then shook hands with Sheil very kindly, no jot of courtesy abated because she was her age, but she went white. I almost got up. His eye was on me. It was my unfair advantage. I balanced my cup, and somehow put my plate in safety. Inside me I was shouting, "Don't you remember? *It's Sheil.*"

Sir Herbert said, "Mildred, I'm going to ring for some more tea. Mine is a little cold; I'm afraid I was rather late," and Sheil caught my eye and considered the remark, her head on one side. I made the excuse of cakes the opportunity for leaning over her.

"He's got to *say* things. All by himself," I reminded under my breath, and the strained look on her face passed.

"But—he's being rather a *pompadour*," she whispered.

"Then make the most of it. You know he 'pomps.' Think of the scene he had with Katrine last week!"

Sheil laughed aloud. Lady Toddington put a plate down, abruptly, and Sir Herbert came over to us, swept off his pince-nez, at which gesture Sheil beamed.

"I believe I have to thank a certain young lady for a bunch of violets. It was very sweet and kind of you."

Sheil leant forward, earnestly. "Did you show them to Henry?"

"Henry?"

"She means Mr.——, I've forgotten his name. Your Associate," I put in, helplessly.

"Nicholls," prompted Sheil.

"Mathewson. No. I don't think I gave him the opportunity. A lady's gift, you know. . . ."

"Katrine said he'd say you oughtn't to accept them, and that I was a Very Strange Young Person. But Katrine isn't interested in him. She doesn't know what a dear he really is," Sheil explained.

"He is a very charming fellow," admitted Sir Herbert.

"Isn't he!" said Sheil. "It must be so more than wonderful for you to have him choose you your favourite lunch things. Is he very disappointed when you go out to the Garrick or the Athenelium?"

Sir Herbert suddenly shook. "I should think he's thankful to be rid of me. I'm rather a terrific old party, you know."

Sheil nodded. "You always say that."

"But I don't lunch out very much." (Here I forgot my policeman *rôle*, and leant forward myself.) "Sometimes I just have a chop sent in to my room, but far more often I lunch in the Judges' Mess. The A.B.C. does the catering."

"Yes," I answered, "cod and shrimp sauce, one-and-two the plate."

Sheil beamed again. "The lambs' tongues are one-and-two as well. *We* think they ought to be tenpence. But perhaps the Law tongues for the Judges are special and different."

"Dear me," responded Sir Herbert, "you've been reading the menu in the hall."

"Oh yes. Deirdre always tells us what you've

had, only of course she thought the menu was only for barristers and people that it didn't matter what they ate. You see, we never thought of *you* and boiled cod."

The wintry smile was very kind. "My dear, I assure you I eat the most ordinary things."

"Mother says you do, but it's wonderfully difficult to believe." Here the maid came in with the tea, and Sheil concentrated upon her. "She's not very like Henderson," she mused, "but that doesn't matter a terrible lot." Ming waddled in, but to her, forewarned, he was so much dog with no element of surprise. Sir Herbert asked her "if she had some pet?" and the formal, familiar phrasing, together with his outrageous ignorance of Crellie, caused in both of us a Freudian "conflict," and I thought it was probably time to steer the conversation from anything unfortunate. Sheil, in her present state, was capable of describing his habits after a full meal. . . .

"Yes. Crellie. A wire-haired terrier," I replied, and at this insane description Sheil looked reproachful. She put a little paw on his knee. "Does Ming do anything interesting?"

"No," answered Sir Herbert, promptly.

"We thought perhaps he wouldn't, though

Katrine said she was certain he tooled leather, or hammered on copper. It's Bottles we really love, you know."

"Bottles? Bottles of what, pray?"

"Your Bottles. The fox-terrier. Does he still go for walks with you round the Square after dinner?"

I waited and let them have it out. There was nothing else to do. It had to come, sooner or later.

Sir Herbert put his hand over hers. "Aren't you confusing me with someone else, dear?" Sheil's eyes hardened, and he looked anxiously at me. I urgently sent him his cue, and he seemed to recognise an S.O.S.

"Bottles . . . m'm . . . what a delightful name for a dog! I feel I have missed a lot in not having a Bottles. And what does Crellie—is it? do?"

"Oh, nothing," answered Sheil distantly.

"He's rather High Church," I said, recklessly, "and after he was the Pope, he used to take the services at St. Albans, Teddington, though it never quite came down to confessions."

Sir Herbert made one of his Bench faces, and then shook again.

"A Dominican," he suggested, "a watchdog of the Lord. Well . . . I can conceive that to confess to a terrier would be better than silence, if one loved the beast."

"I don't want to be rude, but I couldn't confess to Ming," Sheil piped.

"Whyever not?" asked Lady Toddington, who was busy conducting a temporary vacuum with mother. "He's a temple dog!"

"Bravo, Mildred!" answered Sir Herbert, dryly, and her face grew pink.

"Well—he is!"

"And don't say 'whyever,'" I murmured, not daring to catch anybody's eye.

"Well, what I always think is: there's nothing like a dog for company," announced Lady Toddington, and at this I hastily looked out of the window and dragged Sheil to it as well. "A man with a funny hat," I quavered aloud, giving her a hard pinch, and we surveyed the empty street and went on laughing. But Sir Herbert joined us. "I see no such person," he remarked austerely. "He's gone," I answered firmly.

"And aren't you coming to talk to me, Sheil?" asked Lady Toddington.

Sheil went at once. I'm always so thankful that "in spite of all temptations" she isn't a little drawing-room beast. Meanwhile, much as I love her, I had got Toddy to myself.

CHAPTER XIV

IT was very difficult to believe that he was so near to one that one could touch him. All the others have been so diversely inaccessible. And, for the first time, there were p's and q's to be remembered, and one's age telling against one.

"My very dear child" . . . he'd said that so often and written it, in his letters. And now I was, I suppose, Miss Carne.

And then I looked him in the eye, and saw that I wasn't doomed to that. Something was coming.

He said, "Did I hurt your sister's feelings about the dogs?"

"It's too long to explain. But we forgot you didn't know about Crellie and Bottles."

"We?"

"Yes. She forgot more than I did, of course. But I'm in it, too."

He absently swung his pince-nez. "A game?"

"Let's call it that."

"It sounds full of possibilities. A game . . . m'm . . . and I didn't play nicely. One would like to please her. What a singularly attractive small person it is! But why she is interested in me is really baffling."

"You mean: 'To-day, I gave the mother of an unwanted baby penal servitude for throwing it over Blackfriars Bridge, and yesterday I sent a man to the gallows.'"

"Entirely so."

"But, don't you see that that doesn't matter to us! It's part of your business——"

"But when, so to speak, is my business not my business? When, as it were, does Mathewson presiding over my lunches come in? And the dog——"

"*Crellie!*"

"I was alluding to Bottles," he countered brusquely, and I laughed in his face, "Where do they fit in?"

"All the time. One can't always tell when. They just happen."

"How did you know that I am attached to Mathewson?"

"That grew. But it was also plausible, wasn't it? And it was all my idea," I added proudly.

"Ah . . ." and Sir Herbert thrust his head forward and scanned me with those tired, kind, brown eyes. "Tell me, what else do I do?"

Here I deliberately pulled his leg; gave him a reasonably adequate *résumé* of his public engagements for the past six weeks, together with the *bons mots* he had dryly delivered, the first nights he had attended and the barristers he had snubbed, at which his face relaxed grimly. "You dangerous lady! But that wasn't quite what I meant."

I smiled back. "Of course I know that. Well . . . there's a lot of it." (*And some of it you can't be told, Toddy*).

"For instance, have I ever done anything disgraceful?"

"Tut, no! Never. You've had scenes, of course, with Dion Saffyn——"

"And who——?"

"A pierrot. He's dead."

"Why did we disagree?"

"Because you thought he wasn't fit company for us."

"I was perfectly right!"

"No. Not that time. You weren't clever about Saffy. He was a dear. And Sheil hasn't been told he's dead, so he still comes in to meals."

At last, Toddy was beginning to look at me with the expression I had had from him so often before. Knowledge . . . intimacy . . . infinite whimsical wisdom. The relief of it made me grip the acorn of the blind.

"I see . . . and who else do I know? Am I on terms with anyone alive, for instance?"

"Rather! Sir Horatio Sparrow."

"Ah, come now! That's better. He is, as a matter of fact, a great personal friend of mine."

"Is he? How heavenly!"

He stood thinking. "By the way, is my wife in this?"

"Yes."

"M'm . . . I'm glad of that," said Toddy.

And then I glanced across the room and saw on Lady Toddington's face the wife-look. And suddenly I was Miss Deirdre Carne.

I don't remember that we said anything as we walked home. I wondered whether Toddy would ring us up, as usual, last thing at night, and it then occurred to me that our actual acquaintance with the Toddingtons might put a stop to all that. It might be going to alter all the old, familiar things. We even might be going to lose more than we had won . . . it rather depended on mother and Sheil. I could go on, of course . . . I was irrationally despondent. Having to leave Toddy like that, and be ushered out into the Square, was as painful and ridiculous as a lovers' quarrel. And if Lady Toddington was going to turn into affronted conjugality on us, we should have to make a drastic overhaul of the entire story. She had, I seem to remember, shown signs of restiveness in the past, when Katrine and I kissed him and called him an Old Pet, but on those occasions there was always mother to pick up the pieces and mend the breach in a jiffy. The Toddingtons have no "s." no "d." or they'd figure in *Who's Who*. Was the attraction going to be Sheil? And was I going to mind too badly if it were? But one would adore to make them happy. Toddy has done so much for one that he will probably never know. And Mildred has given one so many laughs! Was it possible that knowing the Toddingtons might be going to be just a matter of "new friends"? Is it only selfishness to tinker at their personalities? But we've guessed right so often that it may be justifiable. On more than one occasion we've sent Toddy overnight to some public function, and found in the morning papers that he was actually there, or at something amazingly similar. And there is the sheer scavenging: for, once you are caught in anybody's current, you are apt to be drawn towards people who already possess knowledge. There was that girl I met at the Florences'—an Academy friend of Katrine's. Her mother had once rented their

seaside house at Birchington to the Toddingtons,
and Lady Toddington hadn't liked the bathroom having no geyser.

"I like Mildred," said mother, that night.

"Good thing, isn't it? Because one always
has," I answered. "What did you talk about?"

"Oh, you and Sheil mostly. Well, you got
Toddy, anyway. What did the old darling say?"

"My dear, I told him about the Saga."

"You *didn't*!" Mother put down her cigarette.

"Bits."

"Lor! *Lor*!"

"And I think he catches on." Suddenly I was
full of happiness and, as I always do, rushed to
the piano and improvised a dance tune. (A
year later, I sold it for more than I'd ever earned,
which only goes to prove what a basic ass the
world really is.)

"I like that," said mother. "Do go on going
on."

And then Miss Martin was in the doorway.
Mother hastily crushed out her stub and I
stopped at once.

"Oh, Mrs. Carne, I'm so sorry to trouble
you, but could you come up to Sheil?" We
were both on our feet. "She's being *so* difficult,
this evening." At that, we both sat down.

"Do come in, Miss Martin. What seems to
be the matter?"

Miss Martin turned a brickish colour.

"I—of course she doesn't *mean* anything, but
—it's silly to repeat, of course—but she says
she wants that Mr. Pipson to sleep with her."

"How adorable they'd look!" I remarked,
but catching mother's susceptibly watering eye,
I gave an excellent imitation of efficiency and
left the room to its atmosphere of apologies.

"Anything else?" asked Mrs. Carne.

"Well, when I asked her if she had enjoyed
the afternoon with Lady Toddington, she began
to cry, and became—really——"

"Ah. I was rather expecting something of
the sort," responded her employer.

Over the schooled features of Agatha Martin
flitted non-comprehension, dawning temper,
and resentment. She had had a wretched day.
The unfinished letters to Violet and Mabel in
which cheerfulness must be maintained . . . the
letter from Arthur, confirming his transfer to a
curacy in the East End . . . the secret offer of a
portion of her salary to Flossie. Mabel's old lady
had died, and Mabel was out of employment,
and at home.

Agatha's eyes began to water. Inside, she
was saying to Mrs. Carne, "You are a fool and

your children are liars. Your fault. You are undermining my work and encouraging senseless delusions." Oh, the *healing* of saying that! But repression and expedience said something else, though she was pleased to hear that her voice was chilly.

"Indeed? In that case, could you not have given me some—hint?"

"But, Miss Martin, does it really matter? You know what children are. I was very much the same, myself."

(*You would be.*) "Quite so. But—do you think it is perhaps quite—the best thing to encourage so much pretence?"

(*I know it's wrong of me, but I can't seem to have patience with women with faces like roast hares.*) "Ah, don't try and turn them out of fairyland too quickly. There's all the time there is for coming down to earth with a bump."

(*But, apparently, they don't come down, you silly woman. Katrine seems to be acquiring a little sense, but look at Deirdre.*) "I see what you mean."

(*That you don't! and I wish you'd go*).

(*It's ridiculous, and dangerous. How can one hope for results with the child brought up in such an atmosphere?*)

Miss Martin left the room.

CHAPTER XV

THERE was no engagement for the evening, and
Sir Herbert Toddington joined his lady in the
drawing-room, after dinner. It had been
rather a silent meal; possibly, he thought,
through contrast with the young voices whose
tones still seemed to hang in the atmosphere.
Mildred was being nervous with him. He hated
it. It disappointed him, and she guessed that,
and it made her worse. She was deep in one of
what to himself he termed her "Should She
Have Done It?" novels. Curious how nearly
all women could adapt themselves to the social
side and still remain mentally at a standstill
That little child . . . the pretty thing! Wanting
him to play . . . and Miss Deirdre . . . there
was a companion! The gift of fearlessness,
when one was so sated with perfunctory
deference. It wasn't always easy to shed the
lordship at home, and for the first time he
wondered if he had ever seemed to bully
Mildred? Of late years she hadn't appeared to
be able to get past his manner, though, goaded,
she could occasionally let fly. Sparrow under-

stood her, but then they were old flames and he wasn't her husband. Apart from Mildred, Herbert knew that Sir Horatio Sparrow had a very low opinion of women, whereas Herbert had for the entire sex a curious tenderness and admiration which must have been innate, or his experiences of them in the courts would have destroyed it years ago. For women, he had often stretched the law to splitting point. And then he remembered the boiled cod and the Athenelium, and chuckled.

Mildred dropped her book. Stooping to pick it up, the title caught his eye. *The Life of Charlotte Brontë*, by Mrs. Gaskell. Keeping a poker-face, he restored it. Mildred turned very red. He longed to know how it struck her, but to ask would lay him open to the charge of patronage. Mildred was sensitive about her mental attainments. He used to chaff her, in the old days. Defensively she forestalled him. "Not Edgar Wallace after all, Herbert!"

"So I see, my dear."

"'The poor woman has got glimmerings of intelligence,' eh?"

"Come, come!"

"Come *where*? I do wish you wouldn't use those silly Court expressions on me."

"Now, my dear, don't let us be cross."

"All right. Only you do think I'm a perfect fool, don't you?"

"By no means. I think, in your own department, you are a most able woman."

"That means that I know just enough not to serve cheese-straws with the fish." Behind the pince-nez his eyes gleamed with amusement. "Oh well . . . humour the village idiot. Anyway, Herbert, you must admit that I'm a shade more presentable than the usual Chesterfield sofa your colleagues seem to marry."

"Dear Mildred, do not fight me, if you please."

". . . and now I suppose I've met my Waterloo in the Carne girl."

"My dear child!"

"Oh, I suppose something of the sort was bound to happen." This, her husband thought rapidly, was an example of Mildred's type of cleverness; too sensible to harbour dramatic fears, she was intelligent enough to dread the mental affinity as the profounder menace.

"It would be singular indeed if I started making conquests at my age."

"I don't know. You're awfully attractive, Herbert. You were very plain as a young man, but you've found your face all right, now." She stopped the "Deirdre Carne adores you" just in time. One didn't give girls away, even to one's husband.

"I should have said that I'm emphatically caviare to the general——"

"One doesn't shut oneself up in the library for three-quarters of an hour with caviare," she rapped.

"Were we, indeed, as long as that?"

"You were indeed. Time flying, and so on."

"The old complaint, books, my dear."

"But you can't *talk* about books—Herbert, what *were* you talking about?"

"We were discussing Emily Brontë——"

"Oh, I know *that*." She saw, instantly, that she had given herself away, and stowed the Gaskell Life behind a cushion. "When I came down, you were doing that."

"Please, Mildred! That is a First Edition." Where did you find it?"

"I saw it on the table, when we all left," she answered brusquely.

"I hope we are going to be friends with the Carnes. I should be grieved if you have taken a dislike to the girl."

"Dislike? I'm very fond of her!" She seemed indignant.

"Oh, Mildred, I am glad! I can see how she admires and likes you."

"I thought so too, at first." She ran her hand through her shingle, like a schoolgirl. "Herbert, I—you won't let me be left out, will you? Please . . . I'm so tired of being just a hostess to be endured, and having to be pompous and no fun. I *like* fun, Herbert, and the Carne girl is fun and she seemed to be fond of me, and I thought there's someone at last to take about and make a fuss of and have silly jokes with that aren't witty and so clever one can't see the point, and who won't score off one when one splits infinitives. And little Sheil . . . and then I saw it was really going to be all you, and I was stranded again. Have Deirdre as your own property, but—let me in on things sometimes." A large tear rolled down her nose.

Toddington, astounded and profoundly touched, came over to her, put his arm round her.

"Dear Milly-Mill, of course you are in everything. I know, you see. Miss Deirdre told me."

"Eh?" she sniffed, her head hidden on his shoulder.

"My dear, we figure in a family saga. I mean, they've got a story about us," his face wrinkled with amusement, "and you're well and truly in it."

"What do I do?" she asked eagerly.

"Just what I asked about myself. I don't know, yet, the full scope of *your* activities (we must find that out gradually), but my own include a singularly helpless dependence upon Mathewson, who chooses all my luncheons for me, plus ill-bred scenes with a defunct pierrot."

Lady Toddington gave a scream of laughter.

"I've got a better one than that!—though Sheil was careful to explain that they didn't *really* think it happened. It appears that once you refused to join in the Judges' Michaelmas Term procession, and dug a burrow and hid in it with only your head out and a mushroom on your wig.

"And they call you Toddy. And me Lady Mildred."

He swept off his glasses. "But, let me understand you. About the mushroom. Why a mushroom?"

"So as not to be *seen*, you old silly! You were part of the landscape, with a mushroom on. Oh mercy! I saw that at once!"

"Hah. And was I not discovered?"

"Never!" she answered triumphantly. "Herbert, *have* you been ringing them up every evening, or is that part of the game, too?"

He looked at her slightly harried face, and shook.

"I really believe I must have. When did I first start telephoning?"

"I don't know. It sounded like a long time ago."

"Then let's not question it. . . . Mildred, we've been missing a lot of good times, haven't we?"

"By Jove, my dear, we have!"

He began to walk up and down the room with the famous stiff gait with which he entered his court before bowing like a jack-knife to the jury.

"You know, I dropped a brick, this afternoon at tea. Brick . . . m'm . . . a witness said that the other day, and it struck me as a most felicitous expression . . . brick. . . ."

("Oh do go *on*! Everybody says it.")

"Well, it seems that we have a dog called Bottles——"

"Yes, yes. I heard that." She was fidgeting with impatience.

"You did? Well, I was slow about the whole situation, with the little child——"

"Oh *Herbert*, you old juggins!"

"I know. I'm extremely sorry. . . . Do you advise the purchase of a terrier whom we can call——"

"That's no good, dear. It wouldn't be the

same. I can't explain why, but it wouldn't.
We'll all have to wipe out Bottles. I suppose
she didn't say anything about Ming, did she?"

"Er——, I'm afraid not."

"Poor old fat Mildred's dog! A washout like
his missus!" But she smiled into his face.

"It's curious how unsatisfactory they've
made one feel."

"Oh, it'll right itself in time, my dear," she
responded comfortably, "and—we'll have good
times, won't we?"

"Indeed, yes."

"Not all Brontës and highbrowism, Herb'?"
Her hands were on his shoulders.

"Heaven forbid, my dear. I want to be
amused! We both need it. I *will* be amused,
too!"

"How nice!"

"Not 'nice,' Milly! Nice means ignorant,
foolish, senseless, fastidious, careful, subtle,
appetising, hard to please, and so on. Dear
me! How can my wish to be amused be careful or appetising? Foolish, possibly, and even
ignorant——"

She tweaked his face. "My darling Herbert—
go to blazes and stop there!"

For a second he looked at her with what to
herself she called his mud-turtle expression:

hooded eye and long upper lip compressed into a thread. Then he shook with giggles.

Lady Toddington said, "I *do* love pulling that pouch by your mouth. It goes back with a plonk. I do hope when I'm your age I shall go back with a plonk, too. But plonks don't come so well in women."

"Now, Mill, stop this nonsense, and confess."

"What?" she answered happily.

"Exactly how the Brontë Life struck you?"

For a second she hesitated, then plunged. "Oh my dear, its all such a *fuss*! I'm bored stiff! I hoped I was going to be edified, because——"

"I know. And you're a very plucky woman to admit it. Confound the Brontës!"

"You won't believe it, but I *am* so fond of you, Herbert."

"I was afraid you were bored with me, Mildred. I don't know . . . one gets set in one's ways. . . ."

"Hurray! Let's have a drink."

"A very small one for me. I can't put away what you ladies do." Glasses in hand, they sat down side by side.

"And now, what are we going to do about it?"

"Ring them up—as usual," said Lady Toddington promptly.

"You're not serious?"

"Why not?"

"It would be a most unwarranted intrusion on so slight an acquaintance."

"Ah, but you see, apparently the acquaintance isn't so slight . . . My dear, we shall lose those children if we don't watch our step."

"M'm . . . I see what you mean, but—look here, Mill, supposing we did act in the manner you suggest . . . what should we say?"

"That does need thinking out, I admit."

"Apparently, it must be something purely fantastic . . . could one, for instance, bid Miss Deirdre and Sheil to tea in Westminster Hall, in fancy dress? Or to play rounders in the Inner Temple with Hewart, and perhaps Eve and Scrutton?"

"Hah! You old pet! No, that isn't quite the line to take. . . . *Isn't* it a difficult game, Herb'?"

"Terribly, terribly."

The lights struck his hair to silver as he pondered.

CHAPTER XVI

"HOW now, you secret, dark and midnight hag," I said, groping my way into the night nursery.

"Oh, Deir', I'm so more than glad it's you!"

I sat down near her, on the bed. "You've been getting wrong with La Martin."

"I only said I wanted Freddie Pipson to come and sleep with me. Don't you think he'd be comforting?"

"Um . . . I see what you mean," I admitted, cautiously. Pipson's erstwhile rivals, a furry cat with one glass eye missing and a rabbit lined at salient points with pink velvet, were cast upon the floor. The cat had belonged to me; I'd taken it to bed every night until I was past thirteen. "But you'd better only say that kind of thing to us," I suggested.

"Why? Is it rude?"

"A little bit. And La Martin isn't us-ish enough to understand, is she?"

"No! She talked as though I'd made a heenious offence."

(*The hell she did*). "Why did you want Freddie?"

"It's because of Toddy. He used to come in and sit on the bed and hug me. But he wouldn't, now."

"Hey! Why not?"

"He doesn't care for me any more. He's *different*! He was 'how do you do' at tea." A warm tear splashed on to my hand. I thought rapidly. "Perhaps he was afraid Mildred would be jealous?"

"It wasn't that. He could have made everything heavenly and he didn't. He's just a stupid old man!" She nearly shouted.

"Sheil! Toddy? Why, he's a darling!" But, again, I knew what she meant. "Now look here, minx and viperous vixen and very dirty doggess," I said, "you're plain cross. You love Toddy——"

"I don't, now."

"——and you're being mean-pigs to him. What d'you think he'd say if he knew you'd thrown him over on the strength of one piffling tea-party?" This seemed to be sinking in, and I laboured on. "He hasn't any s.'s or d.'s, and we've all agreed he'd love them, so can't we be d.'s?"

"But they're so *dull*!"

"They needn't be. Daddy never found *us*
dull, and he was no end of a good fella. He used
to say that for a young woman I was the nicest
man he knew, and once when Katrine had
chickenpox he put an O'Cedar mop on his head
and imitated Martin Harvey far, far better
thinging."

"Would he have liked *me*, do you think?"

"My darling, don't do the Little Orphan
Annie on me. It doesn't suit you a bit. You
know he liked you." I was singularly relieved to
hear the little crow of laughter that struggled up.
"And don't forget: Toddy is a darling. He's
fond of you, by the way."

"Does he love you, Deir'?"

"I don't think so, Sheil."

"Oh, *when* is he going to begin to love us
again?"

I'm rather wondering that, too.

Someone was coming upstairs in a hurry, and
mother stood in the doorway and snapped on
the light. She had that look on her face which
made one tense, a suppressed expression that
Katrine and I associated with trouble.

"*Toddy's rung up!*"

"What does he seem to want?" I said,
relaxing, and surprised at her tactlessness. I
tipped her the face that meant family com-

plication, and, for once, she failed to take me up.

"He's on the phone now."

"Tell him it's time he was in bed," I answered, underlining the peevish note. "Saffy's been upstairs ten minutes."

"Is Polly out?" asked Sheil faintly.

"Yes, a stuck dinner at the Berkeley with some——"

"Come along!" and mother fairly pulled at us, seizing any part of one that offered a purchase.

"What you mean?" I was cross with tiredness; the tea-party and Sheil had drained me. Mother began to put on her Martinesque face, smiling self-consciously.

"He really has rung up. He wants to speak to you or Sheil."

"*Whaaat?*"

"Hurry, darling."

"You don't mean it!"

We plucked Sheil out of bed, and then—she jibbed; outfaced us, valiant, crumpled, tearful. And frightened. I saw the battle and bewilderment in her eyes as mother's manner penetrated.

"You go. We'll follow," said mother's jerk of the head.

"Hullo" . . . I said.

"Ah, Miss Carne, is that you?"

"It's—it's Miss Deirdre Carne speaking."

"Will you think me very tiresome if I ask you to send a message to Sheil?"

"Oh, no, no——"

"Well . . . h'm! I stupidly forgot to mention this afternoon that Mathewson—in short, he most kindly charged himself with the selection of my food for luncheon to-day. It was—um—a very trying case, and he felt that I needed something rather better than the fare supplied."

"How nice of him! But then, he is a dear."

"Nice . . . m'm . . . yes, he is a very capital fellow. So he had a most excellent feast dispatched from Hampton Court Palace, concluding with grapes from the great vine."

"Oh no, Sir Herbert! He never did that. Tit-bits from Simpsons' or the Cock Tavern, perhaps, but not George Five's grapes."

"Oh dear . . . I see."

Rapidly I glanced up the stairs, then put my mouth close to the transmitter. "Sir Herbert, I can't talk very loudly—can you hear?"

"Yes, oh yes."

"Then, that's not quite the right thing. I mean, Sheil knows as well as I do that Hampton Court is wrong. Look . . . tell her about what really happens. Anything. It's the only way, now. If you have biscuits beside your bed at night, and whether you travel First, and things like that. You see, if it comes to that, we're all bursting to know, too!"

"Then, I'm not quite outside the pale?"

"I should say not!" Out of the corner of my eye I saw the descending procession. Oh well, neck or nothing. "Here's Sheil, Toddy," I announced, and was too excited to feel sick. The look on Sheil's face partly rewarded me. I put the receiver in her hand. ("*Say 'Hullo'*.")

"Hullo," admitted Sheil cautiously.

"My dear, have I brought you out of bed?"

"Yes. How do you do, Sir Herbert?" (*Damn all children*).

"'Sir Herbert'? What do you mean?" At the offended tone Sheil brightened. "How do you do, Toddy?"

"I've just had a whisky and soda, and I'm off to bed. Lady Mildred had one too."

"*Did* she?"

"M'yes. She's been reading, and then we talked."

"I see."

"And then Ethel came in and put the dog out."

"Who's Ethel?"

"Our parlourmaid. She gets fifty-five pounds a year."

"Oh, thank you. I don't mind about that. You mean the Henderson one?"

"Ah, yes. Henderson . . . when am I going to see you again, Sheil?"

"I suppose you wouldn't come round this evening, would you?"

"I really am just off to bed, dear. But I will another night."

"Will you *really*?"

"Yes, if I am not expected to meet that Saffyn fellow."

Shrill laughter tickled his ear, and he glanced over his shoulder at his wife.

"You *do* hate him, don't you!"

"I don't think of him. I merely refuse to acknowledge him socially," answered Sir Herbert stiffly, and again his ear was tickled.

"Oh Toddy, you *are* most lovely! . . . Toddy, what colour are your pyjamas?"

With a faint groan, Mrs. Carne leant against the banisters.

"My pyjamas? Red satin with two rows of gold buttons."

"No. You *know* they can't be that. Katrine thinks they come from Swan and Edgar——"

"Katrine? Who is this lady?"

"Ha, ha, har! Shall I introduce you again, Toddy."

"If you please."

"Miss Katrine Carne—my sister. Sir Herbert Toddington. And, it wasn't Katrine who said that about your pyjamas. It was— it was somebody else. May I know what colour they are?"

"Oh really, my dear, I think some are lavender and some green."

"Silk in the summer and silk and wool in the winter!"

"May I ask what night-wear *you* have got on?"

"Oh, just wincey and the blue dressing-gown."

"I'm sure you are looking most delightful."

"Oh no. Not a bit. *Our* things aren't interesting, you know. But your lavender is most lovely . . . please, what was Lady Mildred reading?"

"*The Life of Charlotte Brontë*, my dear."

"Have we got it, do you think?"

"I should say, for certain. Ask Miss Deirdre."

"I'll read it at *once*, if mother'll let me. Is she alive still?"

"No."

"I thought perhaps she might be one of those sort of writers—like Thomas Hardy—who sounded as if they ought to be dead before they really were."

"My dear Madam Sheil, we must positively meet again very soon!"

"Oh, *very* soon!"

"And, my kindest thoughts to Miss Deirdre."

"I'll tell her."

"I must go now, dear."

"Are you yawning? I've seen you do that, you know."

"I plead guilty."

"Then I mustn't keep you another *second*, or Lady Mildred will be down on me like the twinkling of a ton of bricks. Good night, Austen Charles."

"Eh? Am I called that?"

"Oh, not if you'd rather not. It's only my name for you."

"M'm . . . I think I may quite like it. It's a good name. I must be quite well connected. Well, bless you, dear."

"And you, too."

In the drawing-room, the Toddingtons looked at each other.

"Herbert, you *do* look tired."

"My dear, I'd rather sum up for an hour than go through that again. But, I think I've acquitted myself with reasonable credit."

"Touch and go, here and there, eh?"

"Yes."

CHAPTER XVII

"WHAT an old pearl!" I said, as Sheil reverently replaced the receiver. Then I saw mother's face, and knew there was some clearing up to be done before one could go to bed—and oh! how tired one is. . . .

Mother was trying to laugh it off, her way when uncertain.

"Sheil, petty, what *did* he say when you asked him about the pyjamas?"

For a second, the dazzle in Sheil's eyes was clouded. "He was silly with me. He said they were red satin with gilt buttons. I hate that kind of joke. It isn't a bit *like* Toddy. And, of course, it was just as you said, Mammy-dad. They *are* silk and wool in the winter."

We dropped mother at her door, still laughing; I stopped to execute a Spanish dance on the landing, snapping my fingers, and Sheil toddled ahead, singing "*Je connais une belle mondaine.*" From her bedroom, Katrine heard us and joined in the "*Ah, comme elle est chic!*" with brio.

And then, in the middle of it all, Miss Martin

was suddenly with us. Her dun-coloured dressing-gown was adjusted to the last button. She probably has a bad circulation; her face was very pinched.

"Deirdre! What are you doing, letting the child rush about like that? Do you know it's past ten?"

Sheil beamed. "That's the time he always rings up, Miss Martin," and she did a high kick.

"Don't do that. What do you mean?"

"Austen Charles! He's rung up! And now I don't need Freddy Pipson!"

"Be quiet! Stop it at once!" Her voice was shrill.

Sheil stiffened, and everything but obedience went out of her face. This was a voice and manner we didn't know. "Why do you tell stories like that?"

"It's true, Miss Martin," I answered.

"I'm not speaking to you, Deirdre. Go back to bed at once, Sheil."

Sheil crimsoned. "He *did* ring up, and his pyjamas are lavender and green, and he's had a drink and he and Lady Mildred are going to bed."

"And he told me that Mr. Mathewson tried to get him some grapes from the Hampton

Court vine for lunch," I added suavely. I meant to be maddening.

The utterly incredible happened. Miss Martin flung up her hand. I was just in time; automatically caught her wrist. It was a narrow escape, because such a thing has never happened before in our lives.

"I say, we *are* late!" I stammered, and pretended to glance at her wristwatch in my grasp. "Sheil, Toddy's in bed now, and he'll think you a Most Racketty Young Person if you don't cut off, too."

I don't think she'd grasped the situation. I could see by her face that the telephone talk had once more established sway.

Miss Martin and I were left on the landing. Her eyes were bewildered. She seemed scared, and my nerve nearly went when she began to whimper—on one note, like an animal.

I could find nothing to say. One can't accuse a woman so much older than oneself of the kind of thing that she had tried to do.

"You brought it on yourself," she mumbled.

"Miss Martin, you must be crazy."

Her pale eyes became terrified. "Don't say that! If I were, it's you—all of you . . . I sometimes think you are all strange."

"Oh, is that it? But, must you hit me on that account?"

"I have apologised. I am not well."

"You certainly don't look it. Miss Martin, I can't stand on my feet much longer, but Sir Herbert did ring up. Couldn't you *see* we weren't lying to you?"

"No. I never can. It's hopeless to talk to you. You don't understand. Good night."

Mother mustn't be told, because it would upset her badly. Sheil must never know. Katrine mustn't be told because to-morrow is the first of November and she starts her tour, and must be kept well for it.

That left father and Toddy. Perhaps we shall see father to-morrow as it's All Souls' Eve, and he won't get excited and distressed. The dead don't. They are only calm and wise and friendly.

I was shaking, but I wondered that I wasn't more upset. It is Toddy, of course. He is now the Toddy we know and the Toddy we're going to know. Already he's begun to share with me the being the man of the family.

CHAPTER XVIII

IN the schoolroom Agatha Martin sat hunched in a chair. The day was over at last. She even had the house to herself, with Sheil and the servants in bed; the others were at the station. And one couldn't even savour the quiet sanity of the atmosphere, because of last night. She didn't believe that Deirdre had told Mrs. Carne. But that was the least part of it. If one did that sort of thing once, one might do it again. . . .

Crazy. Would that account for her loss of authority with the child? Families were very awful things: showed one face to each other and another to the stranger within their gates. If one left, would last night count in the testimonial? Back to more children, with remembrance of failure to arrange in the new bedroom with one's things. One was never going to forgive the child for that. Katrine was gone, but that still left three—the worst of them. Breakfast, to which one must come down, had been just tolerable owing to the unusual silence all round. There were no lessons because of Katrine leaving. They seemed to spend the day in Katrine's room, giving one leisure to remember last night. It would have been the child, if Deirdre hadn't stood in the way. Then—one hated children? And they were one's bread and butter.

A dull crash. Miss Martin opened Sheil's door. Something in her welcomed the opportunity. . . .

The light was burning. "Sheil! Do you know the time?"

"Mother said I could read a little in bed, tonight, because of Katrine and not being allowed to see her and Freddie Pipson off."

"Did she say you might read until twenty to twelve?"

"My gracious snakes! I was reading about Charlotte Brontë, Miss Martin. I expect perhaps you know all about her. They had a dog called Keeper, and Emily—the cross one—was a beast to him once, and I got fed up with all of them; and isn't Keeper a silly name for a dog? It's as bad as Tray or Fido. Crellie would be silly, only it's short for Creilagh, and that's Gaelic for 'wasp'."

"Will you go to sleep!" Agatha heard her voice crack. Sheil looked at her, astounded. "Miss Martin, when will mother and Deirdre come back?" Her voice was urgent.

"Don't ask me! They are quite capable of electing to go off to Bradford with that Mr. Pipson."

Sheil lay down. One was beginning to be uneasy, so one sang to keep one's courage up.

"I'm the Captain of the Loyal Kitchen Rangers!"

Miss Martin heard that, too, and came in again.

"Sheil, I know how much you dislike me. All this disobedience is part of it, I suppose. Once and for all, be *quiet*."

Was Miss Martin crying? One had never seen a grown-up doing that, and when one had got over the afraid part, one was so sorry it made one feel sick.

"Oh, Miss Martin, you're so tired and I've kept you awake. I *am* sorry! Don't you think, perhaps, if you got back into bed and thought about someone you're very fond of, they would be kind of there? It always sends me off. Have you anybody special?"

"Don't be impertinent."

"Truly, I didn't mean to be; I'm only telling you how things help *us*."

Agatha Martin became singularly like a human being. "I'm sick of your stories. They are all nonsense. You must learn to see things

as they are, my dear child. All this invented
stuff about Sir Herbert Toddington is making
you perfectly stupid."

Sheil looked bewildered. "But—do you mean
he *didn't* ring up, last night? But, I *heard* him."
Miss Martin was so positive, it almost made one
wonder. . . .

"As to that, it may be true, but I want the
Saffyn business definitely stopped. It's un-
wholesome." Agatha was beginning to enjoy
herself. Freedom was in sight. "Just say to
yourself that you never knew him, and that he
is dead."

Sheil laughed. "Oh, poor old Saffy! You
hate him as much as Toddy does! He really is
a live person, you know—I mean, not like
Ironface. He has an office in Leicester Square.
Deirdre's seen it."

Miss Martin took her opportunity. "Possibly,
but the fact remains that he died in the summer
of heart failure, following influenza. I saw the
notice myself. And now, go to sleep, please."

But Sheil had followed her to the door, and
in that second of time she had seen. One wasn't
supposed to show things before visitors—especially before a friend of Miss Martin. The room
was so black. If one turned on the light, Miss
Martin would see it, and come in again. Sheil

cowered. And look at and speak to one in a
way one had never had, that made one's inside
cold. Mother and Deiry weren't in sight, even.
The street was empty, except for a wagonette
with a horse in the shafts, drawn up at the front
door, and another lady getting out. Miss
Martin was talking to the first one, but quite
soon they went into her bedroom and shut the
door.

Crellie! Perhaps he would come up before
mother put him to bed in the library. In the
hall, she heard his growl.

"Crellie, Crellie! Oh, *Crellie!*"

There was a rustle in the hall.

"You must learn not to bite," and a yelp.

Someone had hit Crellie, hard. His toe-nails
rattled on the stairs. He joined Sheil on the
landing, his hackles up, every tooth in his head
showing.

CHAPTER XIX

WHAT horrible things theatrical companies do! And Katrine was beginning to be one of them, so we stood very close to her on the platform and tried, that way, to postpone her loss. We pipsonised in self-defence.

"Oh well, dear, we're here to-day and gone to-morrow, as the saying is."

"Well, bye-bye, ducks, I'll be popping off home now, an' chance it."

Then mother, with a line she had salved from Corney Grain, and that we kept for departures, "Good-bye, good-bye, dear. *Tell mother I shan't want the skirt.*"

We were bright, and rather awfully funny. The pinch of desolation comes before and afterwards, never at the time. I saw the company cat three carriages away; under the arc lights she looked like something found in the Thames, because her make-up had turned blue. Only one of the comedians had the heart to comeed at such an hour. He, poor toad, had a gag of his own, which he half sang.

"I want to *know* when I'm dead!"

Then Pipson appeared, and the world became saner. He stood, bare-headed, talking to us. "What an hour, eh, Miss Carne! Why does one do it?" then, to mother, "I'll drive her to the rooms, Mrs. Carne, you needn't be in the slightest degree—you know!" And mother did know, and they looked at each other, and the whole affair was suddenly an amusing jaunt.

I don't know if I was making something out of nothing, but I got the impression that Pipson looked at Katrine in an extra way. It's so difficult to say, with a nature like his that is gold right through, and would protect the plainest woman on earth if he thought she needed it.

"Hullo, Boy!"

"How's the one and only Gladeyes?"

"Good evening, Mr. Pipson."

"I want to *know* when I'm dead!"

Mother had smiled her limit: she was giving little signs of restiveness. "Don't you think we might——?"

I glanced at her and saw that it wasn't the anti-climax of departure or the bad-luck business that was in question. She wanted to get home.

I said, "Yes, of course. Come on." She shook Pipson's hand. "Well, I wish you a very great success, and may you both come back soon."

"We must both try and click, Mrs. Carne, as the saying is. I tell her to look on this as only a beginning," and to me, "God bless you. Don't work too hard."

"Good-bye, darling. Write soon."

"Oh, *yes*."

But mother walked away quickly in spite of the minutes she might have had.

"What's the rush, lammy?"

"Oh . . . I just thought we'd better be off."

I knew that tone. It meant that mother had her reasons.

CHAPTER XX

WHEN we turned the corner into our street and saw a wagonette, mother stopped hurrying.

"It's no use, now. They've come."

"Who?"

She grasped my wrist, but gently. "It's all right. Keep your eye on the door. We may never see them again. Quick. Look!" A figure was on the step.

"Emily, you have been behaving badly."

"The dog is spoilt, and at times his nature is ill-conditioned."

"The family is not returned. Come, my ain bonny lamb."

The light from the lamp-post showed us, for perhaps five seconds, a small woman, wearing the new long skirt, and a taller figure, badly dressed, with clumsy sleeves that bunched on her shoulders. They took their places, the former after a short-sighted peering.

"Well . . ." breathed mother. She was white, but taut with excitement.

Of course, when we were in the hall, I should

have known in any case that it had had strangers. The house was simply humming with alien personalities. I opened the library door, but father wasn't there. Mother was already half-way up the stairs.

On the landing, Crellie advanced to meet us, smiling and dancing, as terriers do. I slapped his back heartily to congratulate him on our return, and noticed that he flinched.

We made the only noise; there was no sound from the closed doors of Sheil and Miss Martin, and mother said, "Thank God."

I followed her into her room, and we both had a whisky and soda.

She said, "It was Yorkshire, of course."

I saw. It explained much.

"Well, what's your theory?"

"Possibly to satisfy themselves that Sheil was better——"

I shook my head. "That doesn't quite fill the bill, with me."

"What, then?"

"My dear, I think they came after Miss Martin."

We talked, I imagine, for about half an hour, then I left. In my bed was Sheil, and one glance at her hurt me.

"Why, you unmitigated limb!"

She had been crying herself ill, and there were rings round her eyes. "Sheil, pippit!"

"Is mother home?"

"Yes. Want to see her?"

"No . . . I don't want her worried, so I promised myself I wouldn't try and see her."

"I rather like you, Sheil. What kind of matter is it?"

"Deiry, Miss Martin says that Saffy is dead."

I boiled with fury, and that made it difficult to think quickly. I heard myself saying, "My dear, he is dead, in a way. He caught a bad chill, poor Saffy, and I expect it was coming off the pier with Pauline and Ennis."

To my immeasurable relief, she took it quietly. "But, after all, it doesn't really matter. He's as much with us as when he was alive, Sheil. We never saw him in London, did we? And creations like Saffy don't snuff out, do they? He says, 'Heaven is awfully slow, and the dam' angels are all playing old stuff on their harps, and hated it when I gave 'em *Melodious Memories* and *Singing in the Bath-tub* on my banjo.'"

She bored her russet head into my shoulder. "And you mean he'll go on coming in and telling us about everything?"

"Lord bless you, yes. And oh! won't there be scrapping matches now between him and Toddy! Duels, no less, my sweet creature! And we shall have to step between them, in our taffetas and red heels and say, 'Nay, Sirs, I protest I am not worthy this unmannerly brawl. Come, put up your blades!' and things like that."

"Deiry, those ladies——"

So she'd seen them? Staking my luck on the way she had taken the Dion Saffyn *débâcle*, I said, "Oh, yes. They're rather like Saffy, you know." And then, an awful thing happened. She became small with fear; she seemed to grow thin before my eyes. All children, I suppose, are incalculable.

"You mean—they are dead, too?"

"They'll never die, old darling. You see, they've made something that's going to go on— for everybody, not only for us, as Saffy was——"

"Deiry, is *everybody* dead?" It was a wail.

"Not me or mother, or Katrine, or Toddy and Lady Mildred, or Freddie Pipson, or Crellie, the ones who love you best." An idea occurred to me. "What made you think the ladies were dead?"

"She hit Crellie, and the other one—the spectacles one—called her 'Emily' . . . will they come any more? Everything was being awful and angry, and the house felt all wrong, and then they came."

"How 'all wrong'?"

"Miss Martin."

I boiled again: nerved myself for a few words with Miss Martin in the morning. "Then what happened?"

"The spectacles one went into Miss Martin's bedroom and they talked."

(*Miss Martin certainly hadn't deserved this, confound her*). "I see."

"And I didn't hear them come. They were just there. Deiry, I think the Emily one was the one who hit Keeper."

"He probably deserved it. Look here, petty, would it amuse you to sleep in here, to-night? You'll be much warmer for me than the hot-water bottle, and if you go off the boil, I'll pour you back into the kettle!"

CHAPTER XXI

HALF-WAY through breakfast, I began to realise how peaceful we were being, and then the reason suddenly came to me. Miss Martin wasn't at table. I was still raging, deep down, but how terrible it must be not to be wanted! Mother and I were played out, to judge by our faces, and Sheil had nothing to contribute at all. Katrine's gap ached one.

I said, "Miss Martin's awfully late," and then mother began to realise it, too. "Just give her a call, Sheil." But when she saw Sheil's look she said to me, "You go, darling, will you? You've finished."

I knocked, waited, and opened the door. The room was empty. I stood and took it all in. The bed was neat, but seemed to have been lain on because the centre was flattened. All the photographs were gone; the trunk, initialled "A. E. M.," was strapped. Even then I stopped to wonder what the "E." stood for. Eleanor, probably. It's just the angular sort of second name she would get. And now we needn't have a scene! I was merely glad. The next business was how to tell mother, alone, but she was already outside on the landing.

"She's hopped it," I murmured, and threw open Miss Martin's door again, "and I must tell you things."

"But, Sheil?"

I went downstairs and told her that Miss Martin had gone out; took her myself to the schoolroom. Sheil's face was impassive. Oh yes, she would find something to do, thank you, Deiry. Then I re-joined mother in Miss Martin's room and told her everything.

"But, where's she *gone*?" Mother looked round the room. "Cheltenham?"

"Do we wire her people?"

"No. We must hear, soonish; there's her trunk, you know."

"Are you sorry she's gone?"

Mother hesitated. "Well, in a way, I suppose. There's always the breaking in a new one."

I laughed. "Poor La Martin! And that's the best one can do for her——"

"I suppose it was pure funk," meditated mother, "and of course one sees the point of view . . . it was rather awful for her."

"And how like her to pack first! 'With chattering teeth she wrapped the *Daily Mail* about her boots,'" I jibed. But neither of us was amused. This sort of thing had never happened before, except sometimes in the case of cooks and house-parlourmaids, who, as a class, take staying out all night and even being turned out by policemen in their stride, but it struck one as almost incredible when it was a question of Miss Martin. And then, unpleasant aspects kept on presenting themselves. She might be one of those people whose brain became affected by the smallest psychic experience. Your materialist is apt to be always the first to buckle up.

". . . and I wonder *when* she went?"

I shrugged. "Ask me another."

"Look here, darling, we'll have to take on Sheil between us until we're through all this."

"Of course. What do we tell her, meanwhile?"

"Until we hear, I think that Miss Martin is staying with friends——"

"Oh no! You've got it well and truly mixed. That's divorces."

"Then, she's spending the day with a friend who is passing through London."

And so one went on, making second-rate fun for mother to protect her and watching mother being matter of fact and rather hard, that one mightn't be perturbed.

CHAPTER XXII

THERE was a writing-table in the Common Room at the St. Agnes Settlement, and Agatha Martin, cautiously peeping in at the door, sat herself at it, took a piece of the stamped note-paper, and pondered.

Canning Town was extraordinarily noisy, or was it by contrast with the Carnes' house? Dear me . . . the letter was going to be a very awkward one to write, and it was, somehow, so difficult to fix one's thoughts. Arthur had greeted her when she arrived, unheralded, at about ten o'clock this morning. Agatha viewed her recent action with sincere amazement. How had one found the courage to do it? The fear lest the servants should hear one leaving, or meet one on the stairs. Dreadful. But, Arthur had welcomed one warmly; one had, already, a place in his life. ("It's not Agatha! My dear girl, come in, come in! This is better luck than I'd dared to hope for!") And, her hands in his, he had bent to her until she had almost thought——

Then, that talk in his study. "You'll be much

happier here, you know. Work? I guarantee to overwork you, my dear soul."

And it was he who had sent the telegram to the Pater; he who had arranged for a messenger to deliver the letter to Mrs. Carne and fetch the trunk in the Settlement van that collected jumble for bazaars and clothes for his poor. He had gone into the money question, almost robbing the subject of embarrassment. "We aren't able to pay our regular workers, usually. They get their board, cubicle and washing. But if you'll take on the business of acting as my secretary, and generally bottle-washing after me —eh? Ha, ha, ha!—I could offer you ten shillings a week, as well. You'd be more than worth it, to me. And now go and write your letter, and then I'll introduce you to your colleagues. Topping women, some of them." And then, with his hand on her arm, "It's not an easy life, you know. It's the going over the same ground that breaks one, at times."

Didn't she know it! Sheil . . . one put last night at the back of one's memory, and it slid forward. . . .

Agatha poised her pen over the paper. Should she conclude by dropping a hint to Mrs. Carne that the maid had been shockingly negligent about that Miss Bell? She had been waiting in the library, so must have called while the Carnes were at the station. And Muriel had not informed one—Agatha had explained it all in her bedroom. That chilly library, with no fire!

A weird sort of woman, Miss Bell. Very downright. Her reply to one's apology: "Miss Martin, in my experience the governess is little more than an upper servant." Evidently a friend of Deirdre's. She had admitted that she wrote, a little. Agatha had had, at last, to ask her name, and she hadn't liked that. Journalists were probably touchy. And the answer: "But, I am expected. Your employer informed me that I might visit her family." That would be Katrine's departure putting everything out of their heads. But on the whole, a likeable woman. Quite sympathetic, when one drew her out; interested in Arthur's and the Pater's photographs. Pointing to Arthur: "Does he write to you often?"

"Well, sometimes."

"But not as often as you wish. Is the post hour a time of torment to you, too?" Very presuming. Agatha had said, quite sharply, "Nothing of the kind," and offered Miss Bell some cocoa, which was civilly refused. They talked of teaching, and Miss Bell said, quite violently, "It is detestable work!" and then she had looked closely at the clock and said she could wait no longer, and begged Miss Martin not to venture into the cold hall, and left.

Agatha closed her eyes. And then, in the silence, that crying from Sheil that seemed to go on and on, and the voices of Mrs. Carne and Deirdre in the hall. To-morrow morning that must be faced, and the certain unpleasantness: every trifle made a tragedy of by Deirdre and probably by the child's mother, as well. Her very soul was sick of it. Sheil had stopped crying, but they might still come and make one miserable with fantastic accusation. They were already coming upstairs. Agatha instantly turned out her own light. She hardly knew, now, when the decision came to her.

Would Arthur consider that one had been unkind? It would be terrible to be unkind. One had, apparently, wounded, but what? A child like Sheil and a family like that were no fair test of one's abilities.

"DEAR MRS. CARNE,
"I have felt for some time, now, that I have not been making the headway with Sheil that I had hoped. She is, in some ways, unusual, and not, I find, easy to handle.

"I have to tell you that I have accepted a secretarial and social worker's post at the above address which was offered me, quite suddenly. I trust that you will overlook my leaving you, and beg that you will retain any salary due to me as some slight recompense for the inconvenience that, I greatly fear, I must have put you to.

"Will you kindly allow the messenger to be given my trunk? (The name of the Settlement is on the van).

"A Miss Bell called last night——"

One was going to be happy, here. Hard work for definite ends, with Arthur. The distempered walls being decorated by all of us for Christmas; making the wreaths of greenery bought from street barrows, and comparing notes round the stove.

CHAPTER XXIII

WHEN Miss Martin's letter arrived in the late afternoon, mother was so relieved that she said, "Burn and sink the woman!" and wrote her a cheque for the time, and even the fraction of days, that she had been with us. The letter that accompanied it was on the "Of course if you feel you must go" lines, and hoped and believed and also felt . . . and she was Miss Martin's very sincerely.

"And now, shall we try and get Miss Chisholm back? She was a fool, but not a *bloody* fool."

"Wouldn't you give *anything* to know if La Martin spoke to Emily?"

Mother smiled appreciatively, but her determination was fixed.

"Let that sleeping dog lie."

"Couldn't one write to her about something else, and find out, casually?"

"Please not, my dear. It's going to be bad enough with Sheil."

"You've noticed, too?"

"Duffer!" Mother put down the Martin

letter. "What passes me is why Sheil is so afraid of them. I mean, she knows about Daddy——"

"It isn't quite the same thing." I was struggling to express what I felt. "And then, you know, coming on the top of Saffy—and what Miss Martin may have said. She—she had a temper."

Mother winced. "But, Sheil *knew* that Charlotte and Emily were dead."

"—or I wouldn't have told her, of course. But it was the suddenness of it——"

It was no good; I—just—couldn't get at the way to help Sheil. It was there, waiting, and that was all I knew. Mother and I found ourselves on the stairs, making for the schoolroom. Sheil was sitting at the toy theatre, tapping one of the characters against the stage, and her mind somewhere else.

"Petty, Miss Martin has got another post and we shan't see her any more, and let's have a spree until lessons begin again." There was relief in Sheil's eyes, but I guessed that Miss Martin's exit would soon cancel it out, and that she probably didn't believe in the simplicity of the truth. One could see her, calculating. . . .

Lunch and tea were dreadful meals; two

gaps at the table, mother anxiously joking, Sheil almost completely silent, Ironface failing to interest (though her aeroplane had crashed near Valenciennes and she was the talk of Paris), and Dion Saffyn unsure of his welcome, hanging between heaven and earth, poor wretch. One couldn't shut oneself up and write to Katrine because one must be with Sheil, and when I couldn't stand it all another second I said, "Toddy's coming round this evening."

Mother shot a look of reproach at me, and Sheil's brief glance accused me of treachery, with contempt thrown in. As her bedtime came round, mother said, "What are we going to do? If we put her in her room she may be lonely and frightened, and if we put her in your room she'll think there *is* something to be afraid of. Why, you're in your hat and coat! You're *not* going out?"

"I'm going to the Toddingtons."

"Darling, you *can't*!"

"About Sheil."

Mother stood and thought, then let me go without another word.

CHAPTER XXIV

ETHEL admitted me. Her ladyship was out but would be in shortly, for dinner. Yes, Sir Herbert was in. "Miss Deirdre Carne." He was in the study, and looked up with an expression I knew.

"My dear Miss Deirdre, this is nice of you. Now, do make yourself comfortable. There. My wife will be in any minute, now."

"I came because I thought I should find you in, at this time. Sir Herbert, it's about Sheil; I don't quite know where to begin."

"One minute. She's not ill, I trust?"

"It's not that. I'm wondering if you're going to believe me."

He swept off his pince-nez, smiled at me with his old, tired eyes.

"My dear, I have now got to the age when I can believe in as many as three impossible things before breakfast."

"But, it's all rather *unlikely*——"

"Deirdre, in the War there were two young airmen who, at a certain altitude, found a new race in the sky. Dragons. It never became

206

widely known for the obvious reason, though it leaked out in the *Occult Review*, if I remember. Pray go on."

"Then, you do believe——?"

"Suppose we keep to the point."

"Well, then . . . We were in Yorkshire, this summer. We were miserable there. Sheil was ill. The place was near Keighley, and it didn't like us."

"It——?"

"Some places are against one, from the start."

"I see. Yes. I know what you mean."

"We were table-turning one night, and we got into touch with the Brontës. They came through at once. Charlotte said, 'Remember Anne, remember Elizabeth, remember Maria' . . . and then, 'Sheil, go back in time.' And we went, next day. I don't know why I didn't connect Anne and the other two with Charlotte and Emily——"

"They were the elder sisters. They died practically at school," murmured Sir Herbert, absently, "Anne, the youngest, died at Scarborough many years later."

"Yes. I remember. Charlotte said she was dead 'by the North Sea,' and Miss Martin, the governess, thought they were all the queens of England——"

"Take your time, my child. After all, you were on the Brontës' territory. I could cite similar instances, elsewhere. There was the case of a friend of mine who walked right into the French Revolution at a little village called Marquis, near Wimereux. He saw the tumbrils and the *tricoteuses* . . . but I am interrupting. Was it the table-turning that upset Sheil? She is, I suppose, too young to realise the unique privilege——"

"Oh, she was in bed. We didn't think of it like that, because you know what table-turning usually is; fake messages from John Bunyan and Cardinal Newman, and so on——"

"Yet, you left the next day?"

"Yes. *Any* warning about Sheil, from even a spirit——" He nodded, abruptly. "She had one of those low fevers, too."

"Well, well——"

"I'd brought my novel along——"

"Forgive me, but does this bear on the trouble?"

"I think so. Sir Herbert, there were pencilled criticisms on it that weren't there before."

"Can you remember any?"

"'Your thought here suffers confusion . . . we all feel the inherent worthlessness of such a nature as you depict . . . your Frenchman is, indeed, a laughable creature——' "

Sir Herbert looked at me. "I seem to recognise Charlotte's touch."

"I think so, too; but when we got home, the pencil notes weren't there."

"Really, Deirdre, I envy you profoundly! Go on."

"Charlotte asked if she could come and see us. And she and Emily came on All Souls' Eve. We were out, and Sheil saw them both. Toddy —Sir Herbert, Miss Martin had been frightening Sheil. The night before, she'd tried to hit me. She lost her temper because she thought I was still on the Saga about you, and that I was making a fool of her about your having rung up . . . she took it out of Sheil when mother and I were out. She told her that Dion Saffyn was dead . . . and then Sheil saw Charlotte on the landing. Sheil had an instinct that it was Charlotte, and she was terrified. And now, we don't know what to do for her."

"Deirdre, why are you asking me for help?"

I faced that. Nothing seemed to matter much. "Because one always has. For over two years!"

"And, have I never failed you?"

"No."

"How have I helped?"

"Oh . . . you congratulated me on my novel and took me to dinner at the Ritz, and you motored from Bristol to be with us when it was refused. You came to Katrine's term-end show at the Dramatic School—things like that."

"'The first to welcome, foremost to defend,' in short?"

"Yes."

He put his hand on my shoulder. "And now, at last, chance (let's call it that) has given me my belated opportunity to live up to myself . . . this Miss Martin . . . was she upset, too?"

"She's left us. Got another job. She hated Yorkshire, I'm glad to say, damn her!"

"Now, now!"

"She thought it 'weird,' and resented being looked at by the villagers, and a red-haired boy who, I admit, was always drunk."

"Branwell Brontë," mused Sir Herbert.

I stared. "Branwell. Of course. I never thought of that."

"I could shake you! I must go to that Inn, next summer."

"Well . . . that's all. Mother thinks that Charlotte and Emily came to see if Sheil was well again, but *I* think the attraction was Miss Martin. She didn't fit in, either, as a governess."

He joined his finger tips. "There is a third possibility."

"Oh, what?"

"Hasn't it occurred to you that Charlotte and Emily were drawn to you, as a family, by a happiness they never had themselves?"

It may have been his voice, soft yet plangent, or the strain of going to him for help, but abominably enough, I felt tears coming.

"Emily hit Crellie," I stammered. "Is it imaginable she'd come back to do that?"

He wheeled. "I think it is *exactly* what she would do. I've never forgiven her for the way she beat Keeper." He was going up and down the room so as not to see my face. "Very strong characters don't change with death, Deirdre. At least, that's my theory. If you believe they do, you must also believe in the extinction of the good. Extinction . . . m'm . . . I can't accept extinction——"

Lady Toddington knocked and came in.

She took us in in a second, and on her face was the wife look, until Sir Herbert said, "We want you, Mildred." I had to look at her while the courtesies were observed, and after that she kept my hand in hers, and so we sat.

He told her the first part; relating it, as it

were, in words of one syllable, and her eyes
grew round, and at the end she said, "Well I'm
bothered! But you never know, with old
houses," which made me give a gasp of hysteri-
cal laughter and not dare glance at Toddy. And
then it was time for me again.

It was amazingly difficult. The fear of a child
was easy. "But Sheil knows that people sometimes return. There was father. It was the
most natural thing in the world . . . she accepted
it . . . Dion Saffyn . . . Miss Martin upsetting
her——"

"Can't you tell her she dreamed the rest?"
said Lady Toddington.

Her husband smiled dryly. "Dear Mildred!
This is assistance indeed!" On her face was the
hurt-baby look; the fading-out that I had seen
before, and guessed before that. Then, she
seemed to remember—that is the only way I can
describe her expression—and, releasing my
hand, bent forward and tweaked his ear, and he
twinkled and shook and, on looking back, I think
that it was happiness that inspired her, for she
turned to me. "*What* was the name of that pierrot
—the one that Herbert doesn't approve of?"

I had to laugh. "Dion Saffyn."

"Um . . . look here, Deirdre (I'm calling you
that, if you don't mind). Can't you make the

Brontës like him—and Bottles, you know? Oh, how badly I'm explaining!" But the audience of her life was listening. "I mean, *bag* them. Let them join in, too. If you can't run away from them, run towards them. The kiddy must know, in her heart, that What's-his-name and Bottles' adventures are all made up, and we can make the Brontës just as real, and take the edge off the being frightened of them—shut up, Herbert!——"

"I wasn't dreaming of interrupting, my dear," answered Mr. Justice Toddington humbly.

"And I think we'll have cocktails, now, because I'm not clever often, and it never lasts long, does it, Herbert?"

"My dear, I take my hat off to you." He turned to me. "If I interpret her correctly, Mildred means that, for the little child, the fear was due to the fact, that, as far as her experience went, Charlotte and Emily had no past. And that, in short, we must give them one."

"And a present as well; don't forget that, Herbert."

"And a present. Quite so . . . m'm . . . dear me, London is quite filling up, as the gossip writers say! I trust that Emily will not try and control my diet. Her verbal parries with poor Mathewson should be epic."

We sat, savouring this for a bit, and then I had to say, "Sir Herbert, there's one more thing. I'm so sorry, but—you're coming round, this evening."

"M'm? Oh, I see what you mean." He gave a wintry smile. "Was it fixed up over the telephone?"

"Mayn't I come, too?" Lady Toddington's face fell. Greatly daring, I put my arm in hers. "There's just one more thing," I ventured. "Now that we all know what to do, would you, perhaps—would it help if I gave you a few tips?"

She patted my arm. "No you don't, my dear! Let's all make our own mistakes, not anybody else's."

Sir Herbert was thinking. "But, Mildred . . . the Brontës . . . I could coach you up in them——"

"Hark at him! Coach nothing! I think they were a couple of dreary bores. I shall say whatever I feel like!"

She tossed off her cocktail and looked wonderfully young.

CHAPTER XXV

KATRINE and Freddie Pipson are in love. I take Crellie nearly every afternoon into Kensington Gardens to walk it off, and every now and again I re-read her letters.

"MY OLDEST,

"Once again I take pen in hand and hope you are the same. The provinces are plain Hell and the girls such lady-dogs to me that, last night, I howled in the dressing-room, and took my things and made up in the w.c. next door. And even the limited rags one might be having Freddie Pipson won't let me have. I am so pure that I shall surely burst. (I mean things like meals at hotels with parties; perfectly harmless.) Somehow, wherever I go, F. P. is there too, suggesting I shouldn't."

And

"It's simply awful to be so dry-nursed. Last night a party of naval officers took the stage box and sent us in a couple of bottles of beer each (I gave mine to dresser), and they invited us out *en bloc* and I wanted to go and F. P. suddenly came out of the stage door and put me into his car without a with-your-leave, and so on. He then apologised all the way home, and came out with one heavenly pipsonism after another—I must save them all up for you. One of the gems of the collection was, 'I'm well aware, Miss Katrine, that when you're in Rome you must do as do does, but you, if you'll excuse me, are an exception.' I said, 'Don't name it, Mr. Pipson. The girls all think I'm living with you, as it is.' And he said, 'Ah. I was afraid they might,' which left me stymied. I couldn't say 'How rude of you!' or 'The pleasure is mine.' And he sighed and looked out of the window, and he would that his heart could utter the thoughts that arose in *him*— Tennyson."

And

". . . I took your tip, and now often come out with the language the Gurls use, and Freddie Pipson heard me in the wings, and came up to me after the curtain and said he knew it was none of his business, and he was taking a liberty, but it distressed him to hear me, and he was sure my dear mother wouldn't like it, and he felt to blame for putting me in such surroundings. I felt so awful that I told him why I did it, and he took my hand and squeezed it and said he knew, and bought me an enormous bunch of chrysanthemums—the adorable kind with mop-heads. And I'm falling for him with a sickening thud.

"P.S.—There is a three minutes black-out at one part of the show, and my place is by Freddie for the next number, and if he'd been that kind, I might be going to be the happy mother of twins, by now. What a waste of perfectly good darkness!"

The worst of it is that, not only has one got the habit of sympathy with Katrine, but in many ways we are and think alike; so it's hopeless to write and tell her to leave the show and not see Pipson any more. I wouldn't, myself. Running away from love is never any good at all, to our sort. It only deepens the feeling, and it's better to stay and wear it down.

"Really, Deiry my lamb, my luck is right off. Freddie met me in the passage the other night, and I freely confess I was looking awfully nice— I'd have kissed me like a shot if I'd been a man —and then one of those *crises*, as Ironface calls them, arose in which the whole place was blotted out and there were only just us two, and then he looked at me in the unmistakable way and said to himself more than to me, 'My dear,' and went into his dressing-room. (He was wearing a scratch wig and a low comedy dot at each end of his mouth, but some men are never ridiculous). I'm the Captain of the Loyal Kitchen Rangers—with a vengeance. *Oh*, dear! The Brontës: *What* a moment! Tell me lots more about 'em. Poor old Martin! She was *the* original bromide, wasn't she? I think if somebody would quite firmly and politely seduce her she'd feel lots better. There's a rumour we'll be in town for Christmas."

If this is going on, I shall either go to Chatham myself, or talk to Toddy about it. It's not Freddie Pipson that I don't trust, bless him! Katrine doesn't really understand men a bit, and would give them infinitely more in small change than the immoral type, out of the sheer happiness of her heart, just because she wants so little, where the other sort of young woman holds back everything, to grab everything, in the end.

". . . Deiry, *could* one marry Freddie? I can see that he's mine, all right. The thing is that he's so awfully eligible—so unlike the usual men with wives being angry in the offing. And on

the completely vulgar side, he's rolling in
money. . . ."

I could see how Pipson was filling her mind by
the way she barely alluded to the Toddingtons.
And I have done a mean thing: betrayed my
good little friend, and he'd be the first to say I
was right.

I wrote: "Katrine, my Plainest, it can't be
done. We are both born snobs and disbelieve in
marrying out of our class, and sooner or later
you'd begin to resent the situation. I've seen
some of his relations, you know, in the dressing-
room. One of them is called Sydney, and looks
it, and he says 'Naow' and 'Haow' and lives
at Herne Hill. Can you conceive being called
Katrine by him? Or hearing him call Sheil
Sheil? He'd have the right to. Pipson's got a
sister-in-law. She's a small turn and a pestilent
little tick. They'd come and spend Sundays
with you. Could you bear Pipson as a surname?
Katrine Pipson?

"Your children would be a ghastly toss-up.
They *might* be like us, but can you see a
daughter with Freddie's nose? She'd be apt to
resemble him, you know, daughters are always
supposed to 'take after' Papa (you're like

father). How would he mix with our friends? He's a darling and an angel and *we* would love having him, but what about them? Try and conceive Aunt Susan's comments and Uncle Noble's; and dinner-parties together.

"Another thing: Freddie would almost never be home. He spends three-quarters of the year doing circuits, and you already spew on the provinces after only three weeks of them.

"My best of pigs, it *can't* be done! I've known Pipson longer than you have, and I'm just as fond of him as you are, and I don't mind saying that if there weren't so many Ifs about on both sides I'd have loved a week with him at sunny Bognor Regis, in the past. One would enjoy every minute of the day, though I sometimes have m'doubts about (shall we say) the rest of the evening. (Aren't Modern Gurls orful?)

"I know exactly what you're feeling, and I think, I hope, I believe, as we used to say at school when struggling to define '*doch*,' it will pass along."

There. I've made a Roman holiday of my dear little acquaintance, and I only hope I'm right. I could weather it, but there are mother and Sheil . . . one can't have things touch them. But oh! what a gad to marry Freddie! But she mustn't. Oh, what a husband and father and lover were there. I'm sure Toddy would agree with me about the latter aspects; he's awfully fair, even away from the Bench.

"I know you're right, Deiry, curse and damn you. I'd thought out lots of what you say, but not all of it. It's rum how trifles clinch things, but when I'd read your letter I suddenly saw 'Sydney' on our lawn—downing whisky after soda and calling me K'treen. I *know* one must stick to gentlemen, but they're apt to be doocid slow, aren't they? Toddy sounds a live wire, and there was father, of course——"

I was so relieved that I raced Crellie all along our street and called out "Whoops, dearie!" to him, and the constable at the corner said, "Terrible noise . . . *ter*rible noise."

"Bless you, K. All the creatures think you've done what Toddy would call 'the prudent thing . . . m'm . . . yes,' and Saffy, who thinks he's cuts above Freddie Pipson because he makes eyes in white and pom-poms instead of appearing with a scratch wig, is capering with indignation at 'the fella's' presumption in aspiring to you. We didn't even *tell* Ironface.

She's so hopelessly *crême de la crême* that she couldn't take in the mere possibility of such a *mésalliance*. On the French stage, all is *canaille*, unless one is a *Sociétaire* of the *Comédie*. It would be so like her to overlook the fact that she herself sang the *Belle Mondaine* at the *Salle des Odalisques*. The other day I said to Sheil, quite casually, 'Suppose Katrine married Freddie Pipson,' and she said, '*Won't* Austen Charles hate it!' Emily, by the way, treats it with a marble contempt, but Charlotte says that where one loves, one takes. (She's evidently got her Héger on the Other Side). N.B.—Sheil calls him 'Hagar' and seems to think he's the Bible one, so we've put her on to *Villette*."

The schoolroom is beginning to put on its winter manner and to be at its best. Lighting-up time is earlier, and the air smells of wood smoke. To-morrow, I'm taking Crellie through the Gardens and meeting Toddy on his way home. There's only one fly, no bigger than a man's hand, in the ointment, as father used to say. The new governess arrives the day after. Miss Ainslie.

"It's no joke trying to keep one's hands off Freddie, and I think he's finding it as bad as I am. It's *so* difficult to think Sydney steadily when one sees Freddie suddenly in the wings, or on the stairs. I only know you're right when I'm alone in the digs. Perhaps all this is a sign that I'm not really in love with him, but burn me! if it feels like it. The oddest thing is that I feel I couldn't possibly marry anybody unless Saffy and Pauline and Ennis (and even Ironface) approved. And I don't believe you could, either.

"Howjer mean about Emily and Charlotte? Have they joined us, too? What a scream! I always thought Emily rather crazy, myself. How do we strike her?"

CHAPTER XXVI

WHEN Katrine came home, I took her straight off to the Toddingtons. She must share everything we've got. We had so much to tell each other that we could hardly get our breath.

"What do we call her?"

"'Lady Mildred,' quite firmly."

Katrine grinned. "Well I *am* blithered! To think it's really happened——"

"I know."

"And we like her, do we?"

"Awfully. Besides, there is what she did for Sheil. That night, you know."

"And has she really got that bewildered respect for brains that's always getting out of its depth, as we said?"

"Yes and no. She's no fool. I used to be afraid that Toddy didn't appreciate her; it's difficult for brilliant people to be tolerant. Their minds work too quickly, and none of us has a chance when he starts summing up at table, or closing his eyes and giving faint hisses of distress when Mildred or any of us drop bricks. Things like 'under the circumstances'

. . . sometimes Mildred briefs me for the defence but Toddy is apt to rout us both. I never knew how illogical my mind was, until I knew him. Mother and I chaff him, and when he loves me he calls me 'dear child,' and when he's cross, 'Come, come!'"

"How perfect! I suppose you're getting no end of data; peeps behind the scenes, and so on."

"Masses."

The famous Sir Horatio Sparrow is one of the Toddingtons' oldest friends, and he and Toddy are apt to begin the evening in a tremendous atmosphere of one-old-colleague-to-another, and end it by squabbles, placidly referee'd by Mildred, on the most inconceivable subjects. In squabble, Toddy becomes remote and forensic, while Sir Horatio flounces like a bantam and I shiver with giggles in a corner. And Sir Horatio's peevish little face lights with the joy of argument, and his mouth becomes a puckered hole of exasperation.

He writes poetry. Lady Mildred keeps a visitors' book in both her London and her riverside house, because her mother always kept one. Toddy hates the book, and she told me that he once said she had the soul of a landlady and indeed there is one entry which reads, "Hope to come again. Rooms most clean and comfortable, and attendance all that could be desired." This, from a clever, spankable little playwright, who had overheard the remark, and enjoyed the Toddingtons' hospitality at Molesey for a week. Sir Horatio's contribution (date 1889) contains a plenteous reference to the Thames, and begins,

> Methought the shade of Sheridan was there,
> And Tilburina, with her naiad's hair,

and it includes a lot of Latin and compares the sunset on Molesey Lock with similar manifestations over the Acropolis ("Here might I find me peace, meseems"), and by the end of the poem Sheridan is left in his shirt-sleeves. Toddy was looking on when Mildred showed me the book, and shook all over and said, "Poor Sparrow's verses haven't a foot to stand on," and I said, "Laughter in court," and he made one of his lips at me, and said he'd have me removed by the tipstaff.

Sir Horatio sometimes kisses Mildred when he comes in, and Toddy looks at him over his pince-nez and says, "When you've quite done with my wife, Horatio——" and Sir Horatio says, "Haven't begun with her yet, old boy. You must give us time." And last week Mildred said, "Time, you old terror? You've had twenty-five years!"

Lady Mildred and I often watch the two little creatures, toddling reunited to their club, and I say, "Aren't they *rather* sweet!" as the parchment-and-silver figures dwindle out of sight.

She has remembered about Crellie and the confessions at St. Albans, Teddington, and when she discovered that we used to live near there, at Hampton Wick, she took me completely to her bosom. It is part of a past that mother says we are gradually living down, but for Mildred's sake I hoist the skeleton from the cupboard.

My earliest memories are of expeditions filled with the desolate stink of scented rushes, and the sight of Pope's Villa from the towing-path; and the July paraphernalia of collapsible cups and squeaking tea-basket, and spring evenings in the Home Park, pale and malignant, like the eyes of a goat. Mildred's girlhood was spent at Molesey, and her mother left her her old home, so it's all fish to Mildred's retrospective net, and in her eagerness to recreate the past, she sometimes asks me if I remember the Tatham boys, or the Freers—or other persons who were married and fathers when I was still in a high chair. And, by now, the Tatham boys are far more real to me than if I had ever met them, or received their kisses under the suburban lilacs. . . .

She can't understand it. We had, as usual, been deep in discussion of some riverside family her people knew, and I found myself coming out with odds and ends of things about them. There was, for instance, Malcolm Cotton, who slipped down his punt pole under Kingston Bridge into the water, and Mildred was on to that ancient *cause célèbre* in a minute. Then, "But, you say you never knew them?"

I said, "Look here, Lady Mildred, I can't explain, but one can sometimes remember things one never saw just as it's possible to be homesick for places one's never been to."

But here I struck a dead spot. I trailed off into, "If you're frightfully interested in people, you begin to *know* things about them." She shook her head and said I was a funny girl. . . . *I* often think that perhaps there is only a limited amount of memory going about the world, and that when it wants to live again, it steals its nest, like a cuckoo.

Mildred has told me how, as a young man, Toddy would ride over to Molesey from his rooms in Fountain Court, and spend week-ends, and she added, "Of course we knew every one in Molesey society, and Herbert was wild with jealousy at my Sunbury young men," and Toddy, deep in the *Athenæum*, gave a faint hiss, and I tried not to strangle with laughter. It seems that Mrs. Brockley gave big lawn parties, and they had a punt and a small sailing yacht, and I can see it all. And so, in flannels, and I fear a straw hat and even a blazer, and to the accompaniment of tonkle-te-blips from the harps of passing steamers and the light and affable conversation that was current in the 'eighties, the rising young barrister proposed to Mildred Brockley.

We sometimes wonder who he would have married if——

But I *do* love Mildred.

Katrine, her arm in mine, drank it all in. Then she suddenly looked round and said, "Here, hi! I've seen this Square before." We had been round it goodness knows how many times; had passed the Toddingtons' door, talking.

Mildred called out from the drawing-room, "Is that my girl?" and, "My dear, I was just going to ring you about those place cards from Barker."

She accepted Katrine at once. ("Can't have too many of you nice things.") "Well, Deirdre, how's the passion for Herbert?"

"Oh, immense, thanks, Lady Mildred."

"And Katrine? (I'm going to call you that sooner or later, so let's make it sooner.)"

"You must give her time—like Sir Horatio," I answered, and she giggled, took a cigarette and tilted the head of invitation at the box. "And Baby? I haven't seen her for a week. Any news of the Brontës?"

"Rather. Emily's writing a new book called *Swithering Depths*."

"Oh my lord! that woman!"

"*And* it's coming out in the spring. Entwhistle, Lassiter and Morhead."

For a second, Lady Toddington wavered. "Are they a new firm? Oh, I see what you mean!"

Katrine gave a little howl and said, "Oh, you *are* a dear!"

"Just say it again. I *must* memorise it."

We chanted, "Entwhistle—Lassiter—and Morhead."

"I like Lassiter," decided Lady Toddington, "*he's* the brains of that firm. We'll have him to dinner. Tell Baby. And now, tell me. The new governess——"

"Miss Ainslie."

"How's she shaping?" Mildred looked at me keenly.

"Well," I began, "I think she has a good heart."

"That means she's a bit of an ass," said Katrine. "Is she an ass, Deirdre? When people say one's got a good heart it usually means that, just as when professionals tell you your voice is a mezzo-soprano it's only a polite way of saying you can't sing at all."

I had the usual mental struggle I experience in trying to define the governesses. "She's younger than Miss Martin and has 'up-to-date' methods. She's got the sort of face that used to go with being called Gladys, mother says. A kind of *blonde manquée*. She's Bright. She calls the verandah the 'revandah' . . . you see, we've had such a lot of them, Lady Mildred. At Hampton Wick there was Miss Baines-King and Miss Easton, then Miss Chisholm, Miss Martin——"

"'There was Lukin, Mogley, Tipslark, Cabbery, Smifser,'" murmured Katrine. And then Toddy looked in, and I really did have to introduce him to Katrine at last. I could tell by the tiny, cocked glance of inquiry he threw at me that he wished to be cued as to how he and she stood in our scheme, and I said, "Toddy dear, this is my sister, Katrine. You quarrel, rather," and we all giggled. He adjusted his glasses.

"A pity. I seem to be on such unhappy terms with so many of your circle."

"It's only temporary breezes," Katrine explained, "I think *au fond* we are quite fond of each other. But I chaff you, and then you have to be introduced to me all over again."

"Ah . . . present me to this lady, Deirdre."

"Sir Herbert Toddington, Miss Carne. Sir Herbert is the famous judge, Katrine."

Katrine inclined her head. "Indeed? A very interesting profession, I believe. You must quite find it takes up your time."

"Oh, not at all," responded Toddy acidly, "one must have a hobby."

"Perhaps you and Katrine will bury the hatchet now, Herbert," suggested Mildred.

He turned to her. "I should indeed be willing. But—would Sheil approve?"

We all considered this. Katrine said, "Perhaps we might have a very *slight* disagreement now and again, Sir Herbert."

"These sudden, suburban reconciliations," I

murmured. And soon, we had to go, because Katrine's company is playing at the Hammersmith Palace, and she has to have a terrible, sexless meal that's too old to be tea and too young to be dinner at about five-thirty.

CHAPTER XXVII

HELEN AINSLIE set out the last of her photographs, stood her golf-clubs in a corner, and sat down at the table by the window.

"DEAREST MUM,

"I am writing to you in my bedroom, which is quite a nice cheerful one, and the mattress is a spring one, because I've just *poked* it! I look out on the garden—what there is of it.

"'Sheil' *is* her name, not Sheila. It seems it's a place in Skye where Papa (dead) was born; same with Katrine. My predecessor seems to have omitted any sort of exercises from the time-table, so Sheil and I do our 'daily dozen' together. The child is perfectly killing, and I draw her out to get a good laugh. When I first came, I thought the whole family was *quite* mad, but I've sifted the whole business, now, and it's all their fun. Joking apart, they quite made me believe in a Mr. Baffin—or some such name, but when Mrs. Carne saw I thought he was a real live person, she told me the facts, and I had a hearty laugh over that, too.

"I think I am making a hit! Whenever I make a joke at table, they all simply roar.

"There is to be a party on Xmas night, and would you believe it? Mr. Justice Toddington and his wife are coming. Well, I wasn't going to be had, so I said, laughingly, 'Is *he* a game, too?' but he is coming, also possibly a Mr. Mathewson and a Mr. Nicholls, and a couple of girl friends of the Carnes—Charlotte and Emily Bell. When I remarked on this, and reminded Katrine that that was the name of the *Brontës*, she was highly amused, and agreed that it was a perfect coincidence. The Carnes are always full of them. They (the Bells) are friends of the Toddingtons, and I rather gather they met them through them (what a sentence!).

"I suppose I must give each of the Carnes some giftlet at Xmas. It's rather a tax as one has been here so very little time, but they seem to make a tremendous business of Xmas, and the schoolroom is already festooned with paper chains and the tree has come, and we were hard at it with holly and mistletoe yesterday, and had a perfectly killing time, with valiant me on a ladder! I've put up a big bunch of m'toe in the hall, and told the girls (in fun) *I mean to kiss Sir Herbert*, and Deirdre said he'd have me up for indecent assault—for which I shut her up. Joking aside, she goes too far sometimes, but is quite a ripping type of girl, for all that, though I could wish they all read less and played some game. Still, the study of new types has always fascinated me, as you know.

"I think I shall give Sheil *Peter Pan in Kensington Gardens*—I saw some reduced presentation copies in Boots' the other day, and perhaps a shingle brush for Katy, and a box of chokkies for Deirdre. Flowers for Mrs. Carne.

"Yesterday, I came into the schoolroom and found Sheil wrapping up presents, and I saw she had actually addressed one 'To dearest Mrs. Carne from Saffy, Gabriel and Michael,' and when I burst out laughing she got perfectly crimson, so I made some little joke—I forget what, and said no more about it. It is, of course, a case for tact and a knowledge of child psychology, and I already have a planlet to win her confidence. 'Always work with, not against' I found such a rippingly sensible rule at Pridhoe. I took it for granted the child believed in Santa, but, when I offered to be him on Xmas Day, Mrs. Carne said they none of them ever had. . . ."

CHAPTER XXVIII

THE penetrating voices of Katrine and Deirdre came from the floor below to Miss Ainslie's ears as she hovered between bedroom, school-room and night nursery: marking time until the guests should arrive and the gong summon the family to dinner, and indulgently controlling her pupil as she rushed, star-eyed, from room to room, and hung over the banisters. It was a high-pressure job, calling for one's full stock of intuition.

"Who will come first?" (That was Katrine). "Toddy and Lady Mildred or Charlotte and Emily?"

"The Toddys, I think. You know what Emily is. Doesn't care a toot what she looks like, and Charlotte wants her to make a good impresh', and will be working on her till the last minute."

"But I expect Lady Mildred gave her a new fringed silk for parties," shouted Sheil, suddenly.

("*My dear, we're not all* QUITE *deaf!*")

Deirdre hung over the banisters above. "Yes,

237

but you know what they are about presents.
Emily's quite capable of returning it."

"Oh *no*! Lady Mildred would be so hurt!"

("*Not so loud, dear!*")

"Well, *I* think Emily's a runnion!"

("*A what? Look, your fillet is right down over
your eyebrows.*")

"Shakespeare, Miss Ainslie," answered Katrine and Deirdre simultaneously, from above.

"Yes," chimed in Sheil, "'*Anoint* the witch!
the rump-fed runnion cried.' Isn't runnion a
lovely word, Miss Ainslie? It almost makes one
wish one was one oneself."

"Dear me! What a lot of 'ones'! Suppose
you keep off the draughty landing, old lady."
But the bell rang, and Sheil was off in a flash
of leaf-green satin, her coppery hair rising
round its golden band.

"Oh Toddy my true love! Is it really you and
Lady Mildred?"

"Yes, darling, it's really us."

"Then let's kiss each other at once, before
anybody else gets a chance at you."

(*Really*——)

"Now, that will be delightful. But—is there
going to be much competition?"

"No. Only games, unless they worry you,
and snapdragon if the brandy stays lit."

"You pet!" Sounds of kissing.

"Oh Toddy, I *do* think on Christmas Eve your house ought to be hung with little silvery nuts! You'd look so sweet coming out of the door. Isn't he looking pretty, Lady Mildred?"

"My dear child, spare my blushes. Ridiculous! Come, come."

"Oh, you aren't in your wig! It would have looked so lovely with a tinsel star stuck on in front."

They were ushered into the drawing-room, and Mrs. Carne was heard by Helen Ainslie to hope that "the little insect" hadn't been teasing them. Miss Ainslie, her occupation gone, prepared to descend in her gala taffeta with its shoulder-knot of velvet pansies.

Sir Herbert: a small, white-haired old man with a grim face, very like his photos. Lady Toddington: very smart in silver *lamé* with a large, good-natured face.

Deirdre and Katrine on the stairs. The introduction of herself.

"A very happy Christmas to you and your lady," from Katrine.

Sir Herbert bowed stiffly. "You are very good. May I, in turn, proffer you the compliments of the season. (Do I know this lady, Sheil?")

"Yes. Sir Herbert Toddington—Miss Carne."

Katrine and Sir Herbert shook hands.

At dinner, Helen Ainslie found herself next Sir Herbert, who took the foot of the table and carved, very neatly, but surely Mrs. Carne should have done it? Still, of course, he was the only man present . . . no host . . . an old family friend.

Miss Ainslie realised, with surprise, that Deirdre was beautiful, to-night. Commonly, one would select the dark and ivory regularities of Katy, or the bronze elfery of Sheil. . . . Deirdre's looks, decided Helen Ainslie, were contingent upon her expression, and settled to her dinner.

As she looked round the table while the turkey was put on, she also realised what was the matter with the party.

The other guests had not arrived.

She turned to Katrine. "The Miss Bells aren't here."

Katrine drained her glass. "Are you sure?" and giggled. Miss Ainslie hesitated; it was Christmas, but still——

"Would you have any more burgundy, Katy? It's rather apt to go to one's head, you know."

"I don't mind being called a dipsomaniac, but I *do* mind Katy. Miss Ainslie says I'm

soused," announced Katrine to the table. "*Am
I soused, Deiry? On one glass?*"

"Not if you can say, 'Are you copper-
bottoming the bottom of that boat, boy? No,
I'm aluminiuming it, mum,'" responded
Deirdre. "Say it *quickly*, Miss Ainslie."

A little pink, Helen Ainslie obeyed, and sub-
sided amidst general laughter. She turned to Sir
Herbert. "I am so sorry that Mr. Mathewson
and Mr. Nicholls were unable to come to-night."

He put down the carvers courteously. "Ah
. . . was he invited?"

"Oh, yes. They both were."

"Um——"

"But perhaps you have no objection to being
the only man!"

"Not in the slightest."

Something in the tone of his voice made Miss
Ainslie drop a salted almond. Crellie ate it
instantly and audibly.

"Toddy-my-love," Sheil shrilled, "what did
you give Ethel and Cook? *We* said dress-
lengths from Lady Mildred and one pound each
from you."

"Both wrong," answered Lady Toddington.
"I gave 'em each a jumper-suit and Toddy gave
them both ten shillings."

"And dear Mr. Nicholls?"

(*"Sheil, it isn't quite-quite to ask——"*)

"My dear, we aren't on present-giving terms, I'm afraid." There was, at this, a concerted wail from the Carne girls.

"Bang go the golf-clubs," said Deirdre.

"You see, at Christmas, we judges pay into a general fund for the officials, besides a number of legal charities."

"Like the Browbeaten Barristers?" implored Sheil.

"Something of that nature. I have been Treasurer of the—ah—Browbeaten Barristers' Fund."

As the dinner moved to its climax of almonds and raisins and crystallised fruit, Miss Ainslie's efforts to catch the ball of conversation became more fevered. It almost seemed, at times, that the evening was going to degenerate into an effort to cut in anywhere. And yet, one was freely, constantly addressed. . . .

She turned again to Sir Herbert, indicating Sheil.

"We are a little over-excited, to-night. But we're rather killing, aren't we?"

"We? Oh, you allude to Sheil. But—the festival of the children, you know——"

Katrine heard, and usurped him. "Dear Sir Herbert, what a bromide!" she drawled.

"Come, may I not offer you the sugar-plums?' He proffered the dish.

Light broke, and Miss Ainslie turned eagerly, again. "*Is* it a mock quarrel? Oh, how too priceless!"

In the silence that fell, she rather believed that she had made a *gaffe*. Katy was looking coldly at Sir Herbert, and he was returning the gaze with a well-bred smile. Miss Ainslie bent her head to her raisins. One could, at least, listen. Deirdre, opposite, her arm on the table, was saying, "—do you know what I mean, Toddy? It isn't that there's anti-climax about Christmas Day, but there's a definite sadness . . . not being able to be in two or three places at once to see what one's friends are doing in their homes . . . and the way the face of the house falls if one leaves it to go out for the evening. It's a sort of betrayal——"

"Age is a shield, Deirdre. It 'larns one' to take things as they come. It's—I don't speak personally—typical of youngness to grab——"

Katrine to Lady Toddington: "I do so awfully hope that in spite of my complex with Sir Toddy, you're going to adopt me too."

"My dear, I'd adore to. Run in whenever your lovers throw you down and we'll see if we can't spike their guns, between us. I've no end of nice young men up my sleeve, only waiting to tumble all over themselves about you and Deirdre. Only, try not to marry them all too soon, because *I* want to be noticed, too!"

"You dear! . . . but I'm only just over a low comedian——"

"You mean that what's-his-name we saw in your revue the other night?"

"Yes. Am I a cad to give it away? Somehow, I feel one could out with things, to you. Deiry and mother and I understand each other too well; but with you, one would get a new slant on life——"

Incredulous, Miss Ainslie, cautiously raising her head, saw the eyes of Lady Toddington become unmistakably wet. She jazzed it off.

"Herbert! I've just had the compliment of my life."

"Good, dear. May we hear it?"

"No. Eat your almonds."

("*And yet, it's a very cheerful party,*" Helen Ainslie told herself. "*All the ingredients are here——*")

"——don't you agree with me, Miss Ainslie?"

"Pardon, Lady Toddington?"

"I was saying that I think all you girls ought to be made love to before settling down by men

from every profession—from earls to panto-
mime dames. It's the only way to learn."

"My dear Mildred! let nobody indict your
education in that respect!" Sir Herbert leant
back, eyes crinkled with sardonic amusement.

"Eat your nourishing nuts, Herbert. What
I mean is, that it must make a person one-
sided to have only been kissed by gentlemen."

"I'd love an affair with a dame," agreed
Deirdre, shouting above the laughter.

"Pass the chocolates along to Miss Ainslie,
Sheil, petty," prompted Mrs. Carne.

"I've kissed Freddie Pipson *and* Toddy,"
piped Sheil, obeying.

"You little lamb!" Lady Toddington blew
her a kiss.

"Tell me, Miss Ainslie, are you a believer in
the methods of Montessori? My wife tells me
that you are very modern——," Herbert Toddington leant to Helen Ainslie. But she was
already recovering; the "all you girls" of Lady
Toddington and the sane camaraderie of the
crackers made her herself again, and quite soon
she had whipped on a Chinese hat, and, making
a funny face for Sheil, cried, "I'm the Jam of
Tartary. Allah!"

"I don't think it's very like a jam tart,"
answered Sheil, interested, "it's shaped more

like a muffin." Sir Herbert privily shook, and his wife muttered, "I shall die."

And then Katrine, adjusting a tiny straw hat, said to Lady Toddington, "Meet Mr. Lassiter."

"How do you do, Mr. Lassiter. I've always wanted to know you."

"Oh, *who*——," began Miss Ainslie, but Deirdre had already swept her away.

"Emily says he is 'a just though shallow man,' and when I asked Charlotte if she liked him, she said, weighing her words, 'I do and I do not. His principles are unpolluted, but he is a great quiz.'"

"What about your novel, Deirdre?"

"Well, Toddy, I've had the courage to rend it in twain, thanks to Charlotte. You remember her pencilled comments?"

"Of course. I was deeply interested."

"Well, I have done all she suggested. Oh, if she had written more!——"

"——you must pull a cracker with me, Miss Ainslie! . . . there, you've got it! That goes much better with your hair. How I envy you being fair!" Lady Toddington swept the spent cracker aside and nodded, smilingly. Sheil squeaked at the bang, then, weaving her way to the foot of the table, she reverently fitted a jockey cap on to Sir Herbert's head, placed a

serpent ring upon his finger, kissed him upon
one shaggy eyebrow, and announced from a
slip of paper in her hand,

> " Oh fairest flower of all the flowers that bloom
>   Thy mirthful glance has sealed my happy doom."

"That's bigamy, Herbert."

"No, Mildred. At most it is alienation of
affection."

"Charlotte's got a ripsnorter," announced
Deirdre.

> " Fear not, fond heart, but love will come
>   And claim you wheresoever you may roam."

"Snakes!"

"Well, it's not very much worse than *her*
poetry——"

"Let's do one for all of us."

> " There at the table-end sits little Toddy . . .
>   His shirt is linen . . .
>   . . . and his pants are shoddy."

"Thank you, thank you, Miss Carne. Highly
humorous, I am sure, if wholly inaccurate."

"We can't give you a motto, Miss Ainslie.
There's no rhyme to fit *your* name."

"Shall we go and light the tree?" suggested
Mrs. Carne, a little hastily.

CHAPTER XXIX

("*Oh, a most successful party*," Helen Ainslie told herself. But one had to go on asserting it).

In the glowing drawing-room she instinctively gravitated to Lady Toddington. She had fully intended to exchange ideas with Sir Herbert, but there it was.

The tree, dominating the room, sparkled, its base banked three-deep with packages. Helen Ainslie, doing rapid mental arithmetic, discovered amazement, then, remembering her own surprise in store, was consoled. Also, she herself was included, lavishly. The individual presents received, her arms became piled with what might or might not have been afterthoughts, and which the Carnes lumped together under the general heading of "dirts." The silk sports coat from Mrs. Carne, the fur and leather gauntlets, sports stockings, and béret from the girls. And chocolates, notepaper, eau-de-Cologne, a tiny glass maple tree. Dirts . . . how killing.

"The dog will be sick," she observed to Lady Toddington.

"Oh well, let him enjoy himself. It's Christmas." Lady Toddington smiled at Crellie as he sat chewing chocolate caramels and occasionally becoming inextricably welded, upon which he put the top of his head on the floor and stood in the roof of his mouth. Disposed round him were a drinking bowl with a picture on it, a new collar, a net stocking full of toys and a "small mixture" in the toe, a serge pillow made by Mrs. Carne and embroidered "C.C." in one corner and "R.I.P." in the other, a rubber bone, the packet of caramels and a mechanical mouse. The Carnes had also jointly contributed a religious calendar.

Helen Ainslie, reconstructing the evening, would perhaps date the moment that harassment definitely set in from the response of Lady Toddington about Crellie. For the Carnes, their personal *pièces de résistance* distributed, were still passing each other packets with remarks that one never quite seemed to catch.

"From Ionie——"

(*Or was it "irony"?*)

Then Deirdre, coming up to Sir Herbert's chair and presenting a book: "From Charlotte, Toddy dear." And Sheil, leaning against Lady Toddington and watching Mrs. Carne as she drew yet another parcel from the back of the tree and gave it (*with a rather peculiar look*) to her guest.

"That's from Emily."

"Oh, you two darlings! And I didn't bring anything for her."

"You *did*! Look at the things you and Toddy gave us! Besides, she wouldn't have liked it, you know. They're very queer about presents, Lady Mildred."

"They had so few, poor wretches," said Mrs. Carne, "it must have made them rather *farouche*." Here she smiled self-consciously at Helen Ainslie, and quickly snipped a chocolate fish for her from the boughs.

On the other side of the tree, Deirdre and Katrine were heard by Miss Ainslie to proffer unknown gifts from Mr. Saffyn (*it wasn't Baffin*, then).

"—and Polly sends these, with her warmest regards."

"Then she *is* miffed about not being invited to-night! She'd have sent her love, if she wasn't." Laughter . . . a Pauline and an Ennis . . .

Miss Ainslie rose. Her moment was at hand. Her last parcel was balanced on the pot in which the tree stood; she annexed it, beaming. Katy had been so awfully pleased with the shingle brush, and Sheil had thanked her so earnestly for *Peter Pan*. . . .

She put the packet into the child's hands. "That," she announced, "is a little remembrance from Henry the Eighth," and burst out laughing.

Deirdre came forward quickly. "Stout fella," she approved, casually.

"Oh, Miss Ainslie, *how* kind of you," said Mrs. Carne. Katrine gave a high, hysteric giggle.

Sir Herbert said, "Dear me. A typical gesture where fair ladies were in question."

Lady Toddington murmured, "There now! I wonder whatever it can be?" and looked slightly worried.

Sheil thanked, her expression a blank. She had turned crimson. Crellie hicupped.

Helen Ainslie found herself beginning to babble. "Oh yes. He specially asked me to choose it for you when I met him in the High Street. So you open it, old lady, at once, if not sooner, and don't keep His Majesty waiting." Again Sheil's thanks, and in the conversation which sprang up, she found herself and her pupil making for Lady Toddington; in a minor way, it partook of the nature of a race to the goal of this pleasant, cheerful lady. . . .

Lady Toddington instantly put both arms about the child. Helen Ainslie, wondering what remark was going to emerge, opened her lips.

Lady Toddington said, "I saw the Brontës, yesterday."

Miss Ainslie closed her mouth. Deirdre said, "Where?"

"In Woolworth's." Lady Toddington kissed the top of Sheil's head.

"A moment, Mildred. Would they have the means—to say nothing of the inclination—to purchase Christmas goods? Can one *see* them in such a shop?"

Helen Ainslie looked at Sir Herbert closely. He was perfectly serious, interested, argumentative, finger-tips joined. She thought better of the laughter she had been ready to expend. If one laughed, there was no knowing how the party would take it. That was how it seemed.

"*I* can," said Deirdre. "They'd be after the dreary things—basins with linen tops for lifting out. The aunt with the pattens wanted 'em. Besides, it depends whether they went to Woolworth's after the publication of *Jane Eyre* or before. Charlotte'd have lots to splurge with if it was after."

"Oh, how lovely!" breathed Sheil, her head in Lady Toddington's neck.

"You don't need much money for basins," objected Mrs. Carne.

"But, we've only Deirdre's word for it that those were the desiderata," responded Sir Herbert caustically.

"The *what*, Toddy?"

Sheil cocked her head. "You do know such uncommon words."

"I mean, my dear, the objects required."

"Well, *I* like the thing you said before, best. Anybody can require objects."

"You're all wrong, and it wasn't basins, and we must be off, Herbert."

"Oh, tell what it was!"

"Darling, it was writing-pads. And Charlotte bought a hair-net. Mauve. Quite hideous, poor girl. Come along, Herbert."

"Did they like Woolworth's?"

"Ask Deirdre."

"No." Deirdre nipped a smoking wick on a lower bough. "Emily had one of her difficult fits right in the middle of the haberdashery, and Charlotte wrote to Miss Nussey: 'It was a queer shop, much favoured with their custom by a class which I do not think to be our own. The attractions, my darling—no, I *will* not be sentimental—the attractions, then, are lights, variety of articles displayed, music, cleanliness and warmth (from whence obtained I do not know), but proving an evident lure to these families who know no better. . . .'"

Sir Herbert's eyes gleamed as he bade Miss Ainslie good-night, and Lady Toddington advanced and shook her hand, with some conventional remark. Miss Ainslie did not follow the party into the hall. But the voices were audible.

"Mrs. Carne, you're a genius about parties. Wish I had the touch! . . . before the longer days are here, and then you must all come down for stays at Molesey. There's a canoe for you, Baby."

"—then you will bring the manuscript and we will go over it together . . . lunch next Saturday."

"—only au revoir, then."

"Oh, look at Crellie! He's simply *biffing* down the road. Mother's own bolster!"

"—lovely——"

Thanks, thanks, thanks. Evident perception of the hall mistletoe. A great deal of laughter and kisses.

CHAPTER XXX

IN her bedroom, Helen Ainslie was firmly pacing up and down. From the table in the window to dressing-table opposite, and turn. Her presents were neatly stacked. Extraordinarily kind. Everything one had hoped to be able to buy from one's salary.

Then where was exhilaration?

Lady Toddington had failed one, suddenly. A promising and useful friendship gone. Helen Ainslie, arriving at the Henry the Eighth affair, checked her stride, then resumed it more rapidly. That air of contretemps which succeeded the offering of the parcel . . . always work with, not against. But if, so to speak, presents from Henry the Eighth were going to be no good, then what was?

Charlotte and Emily.

Miss Ainslie's cheeks flushed with sundry and deepening annoyances.

The next turn brought her to the dressing-table. Her reflection disclosed hair slightly disordered and topped with a blue paper fool's cap.

With singular asperity she cast it upon the floor.

VIRAGO MODERN CLASSICS

The first Virago Modern Classic, *Frost in May* by Antonia White, was published in 1978. It launched a list dedicated to the celebration of women writers and to the rediscovery and reprinting of their works. Its aim was, and is, to demonstrate the existence of a female tradition in fiction which is both enriching and enjoyable. The Leavisite notion of the 'Great Tradition', and the narrow, academic definition of a 'classic', has meant the neglect of a large number of interesting secondary works of fiction. In calling the series 'Modern Classics' we do not necessarily mean 'great' — although this is often the case. Published with new critical and biographical introductions, books are chosen for many reasons: sometimes for their importance in literary history; sometimes because they illuminate particular aspects of womens' lives, both personal and public. They may be classics of comedy or storytelling; their interest can be historical, feminist, political or literary.

Initially the Virago Modern Classics concentrated on English novels and short stories published in the early decades of this century. As the series has grown it has broadened to include works of fiction from different centuries, different countries, cultures and literary traditions. In 1984 the Victorian Classics were launched; there are separate lists of Irish, Scottish, European, American, Australian and other English speaking countries; there are books written by Black women, by Catholic and Jewish women, and a few relevant novels by men. There is, too, a companion series of Non-Fiction Classics constituting biography, autobiography, travel, journalism, essays, poetry, letters and diaries.

By the end of 1989 over 300 titles will have been published in these two series, many of which have been suggested by our readers.

Also of Interest

WHO WAS CHANGED AND WHO WAS DEAD
Barbara Comyns

"The grandmother cried, 'Don't go yet, tell me more. What about my rose beds?' Her son seized the trumpet . . . and shouted down its black depths, 'Dead animals floating everywhere. Your roses are completely covered'"

At the beginning of June the river floods, ducks swim through the drawing-room windows and Ebin Willoweed rows his daughters round the submerged garden. The grandmother dresses in magenta for her seventy-first-birthday whist drive and looks forward to the first prize of pâté de foie gras. Later Ives the gardener leads a morose procession up river, dragging her to a funeral in a black-draped punt. The miller goes mad and drowns himself and a cottage is set alight. Villagers keep dying and at the house on the river plates are thrown across the luncheon table and a tortoise through a window. The newspaper asks "Who will be smitten by this fatal madness next?" Originally published in 1954, this strange novel with is macabre humour, speaks with Barbara Comyns' unique and magical voice.

THE SKIN CHAIRS

Barbara Comyns

'"Could I see the chairs, please?" . . . "Chairs, chairs. What does the child mean?" . . . "Oh, she means the chairs in your hall, the ones your husband had covered with skin. I'm afraid she is a morbid little thing." She giggled and bounced about on her rickety chair'

Her father dies and ten-year-old Frances, her mother and assorted siblings are taken under the wing of their horsey relations, led by bullying Aunt Lawrence. Their new home is small and they can't afford a maid. Mother occasionally dabs at the furniture with a duster and sister Polly rules the kitchen. Living in patronised poverty isn't much fun but Frances makes friends with Mrs Alexander who has a collection of monkeys and a yellow motor car, and the young widow, Vanda, who is friendly if the Major isn't due to call. But times do change and one day Aunt Lawrence gets her come-uppance and Frances goes to live in the house with 'the skin chairs'. First published in 1962, this quirky novel describing the adult world with a young girl's eye, resounds with Barbara Comyns' original voice.

THE WILLOW CABIN
Pamela Frankau

"He came over to her chair, pulled her out of it and stood holding her hands.

'If I were really grown-up now, I should say good-bye to you and walk out of your life. And yet I cannot bear to go'"

Caroline is twenty-two, gamine and vociferous, neither daunted nor impressed by the prospect of a promising stage career. Then she meets Michael Knowles, a successful middle-aged surgeon, and her career slips into second place beside brief meetings, midnight trysts and the welcome anonymity of foreign cities, as they seek to evade the shadow of Mercedes, Michael's estranged wife. London of the 1930s gives way to the Blitz and the pain of separation and the intensity of wartime does nothing to deflect Caroline's obsession with the three-cornered relationship. In America, some years later, she meets Mercedes for the first time. Discovering an unexpected bond with her, Caroline begins to comprehend her own misinterpretation of the past . . .

A WREATH FOR THE ENEMY

Pamela Frankau

"'In my youth . . . I had an overwhelming passion to be like other people. Other People were a whole romantic race, miles beyond my reach. Not now. I don't really think that they exist, except in the eye of the beholder'"

When Penelope Wells, precocious daughter of a poet, meets the well-behaved middle-class Bradley children, it is love at first sight. But their parents are horrified by the Wells' establishment — a distinctly bohemian hotel on the French Riviera — and the friendship ends in tears. Out of these childhood betrayals grow Penelope, in love with an elusive ideal of order and calm, and Don Bradley, in rebellion against the philistine values of his parents. Compellingly told in a series of first-person narratives, their stories involve them with the Duchess, painted and *outré*; the crippled genius Crusoe; Crusoe's brother Livesey, and the eccentric Cara, whose brittle and chaotic life collides explosively with Penelope's.